He began to kiss her once more...

She shivered as a heady kind of excitement flared in her. That this was she, Amy, who was too thin and who didn't eat enough and who got into trouble in the office for being inept...but for now Julius wasn't her boss, and she let that sweet crazy exultation take her over—just for a few, intoxicating moments...

Dear Reader

There's nothing more wonderful than celebrating the end of winter, with an exciting collection of books to choose from! Mills & Boon will transport you to all corners of the world, including two enchanting Euromance destinations—sun-drenched, exotic Madeira contrasting with scenic evergreen Wales. Let the spring sunshine brighten up your day by reading our romances which are bursting with love and laughter! So why not treat yourself to many hours of happy reading?

The Editor

Lucy Keane first started writing when she was six, got a degree in English at Oxford, and subsequently pursued a colourful career that ranged from working in the wheeling and dealing world of the City to teaching nursery rhymes to four-year-olds in New Delhi. Innumerable hobbies include drinking chocolate in ski huts in the French Alps and digging up Roman drains on archaeological sites. She is an obsessional traveller, and a dedicated researcher into real-life romance...

RELUCTANT ENCHANTRESS

BY

LUCY KEANE

MILLS & BOON

MILLS & BOON LIMITED
ETON HOUSE, 18-24 PARADISE ROAD
RICHMOND, SURREY TW9 1SR

For Sue

*First published in Great Britain 1994
by Mills & Boon Limited*

© Lucy Keane 1994

*Australian copyright 1994
Philippine copyright 1994
This edition 1994*

ISBN 0 263 78424 X

*Set in Times Roman 10 on 11¼ pt.
01-9403-58514 C*

Made and printed in Great Britain

CHAPTER ONE

'WELL, there's Dennis,' said the plump and friendly Jacquie, clearly delighted to be the one to impart all the vital gossip. 'But of course he interviewed you, so you've got some idea of him already. Are you sure you don't want anything to eat with that coffee? The office *is* paying, you know!' Her tone indicated that there would be a blue moon that night.

Amy noted with some amusement the iced bun that was overlapping the edges of her companion's small china plate—Jacquie was obviously celebrating in advance that evening's astronomical rarity!

Then she glanced round the tea rooms with interest—flowery wallpaper, old-fashioned Windsor chairs, and an appetising display of fresh baking along the bread counter by the door. It was an unexpected and pleasant alternative to being asked to wait in that cramped hall of Prior Harding Investments with the decorators about to splatter paint on her head any minute, or wandering the streets for an hour in the rain. If she got the job, she might contrive a few little errands that would take her past the Wistaria Tea Rooms, even though she wouldn't be able to afford lunch-breaks there.

She took a deep breath, trying to steady the continual fluttering feeling inside that told her her future might depend on the very minutes she was living through right now: Jacquie might have been detailed to report back to her bosses on their potential new secretary. Of course Dennis could have made up his mind against her already, but she still had one more interview to go. She smiled at her companion, and opened her third brown sugar packet, pouring the contents into her coffee. Too nervous to eat, she refused the offer of a cake, and then asked, 'How come they've let you take me out like this?'

Jacquie watched fascinated as Prior Harding's prospective employee stirred what must now be a syrupy mess at the bottom of her cup. Amy Thompson was as thin as the proverbial rake. 'Do you always drink it like that? If you don't mind my saying so, you've got the kind of figure that looks as though it's fed on nothing but Perrier and dry biscuits!'

Despite the hint of envy in the other woman's tone, Amy didn't feel flattered. She was conscious of the fact that she'd lost far too much weight recently; surely only someone of Jacquie's over-generous proportions could see hers as a desirable figure. 'I just happen to be one of those people who uses up a lot of nervous energy, that's all. Sweet drinks keep me going.'

'Then maybe you should eat more?' her companion offered, tentatively.

Amy flicked a long dark red strand of hair over one shoulder and took a trial sip. 'I eat like a horse these days but it doesn't seem to make much difference,' she said offhandedly. 'But go on telling me about the job—what's Mr Harding like to work for? He seems very nice.'

'Oh, he's a sweetie really. He gets in a flap from time to time and needs cups of tea to calm him down, but he isn't too demanding when it comes to working late, even when there's a mega-crisis.' Jacquie took a sip of her own coffee. 'Not that Prior's wouldn't give anyone a nervous breakdown—oops!' She put a short-fingered capable hand in front of her mouth. 'I'm not supposed to say things like that in front of someone we're interviewing. But you'll find out for yourself soon enough and you might as well know what you're coming to.'

'Then you think I could be offered the job?' Amy asked with a sideways glance out of slanting blue eyes, trying to keep herself from hoping too desperately. 'Has he interviewed a lot of secretaries?'

There was a significant pause, and then her informant said in discreet tones, 'I'm sure I'm not to tell you this either, but the last secretary just walked out last week—*not*,' she added hastily, 'that it had anything to do with the company! She had some horrendous family problems, and Prior's isn't the place to work if you need time off to sort out difficulties at home.'

That was *very* bad news—but Amy reminded herself that she couldn't afford to comment in a way that might sound negative and get passed on. She had to get the job, she just *had* to! It was the only one that had been advertised for weeks with a salary she could actually live on. Jacquie, unaware of the effect she was having on her companion, went on blithely, 'We're always pretty busy, and all hell's been let loose since the Spanish property deal. But don't worry about the job. I'm sure you'll get it. We've had very few applicants. Wychford isn't exactly a thriving metropolis when it comes to attracting first-class secretaries and we need someone permanent as soon as possible.'

First-class secretaries—and I'm not even second class! Amy thought gloomily, and asked, 'Why is Mr Harding letting you come out to drink coffee with me if you're all so busy?'

'Dennis,' Jacquie corrected. 'We call the bosses by their first names—it's part of the office fiction that we're all equal. He's afraid you might slip off the hook before Julius sees you. None of the other applicants could have coped and he's desperate for someone—most of them were straight out of secretarial courses with no experience at all. Actually, Dennis would have been prepared to put up with that for a while, but Julius wouldn't.'

Who exactly *was* this Julius character? All three people she had met so far had alluded to him at some point in their conversation, but since no one had thought to explain him they must assume his position in the company was obvious.

'I don't quite understand why I have to see this Julius at all,' she began. 'After all, the job advertisement did say it was Mr Harding—Dennis—who wanted a secretary, and he is a director, isn't he?'

Jacquie's eyes opened wide. 'My dear girl, we don't even take on the humblest office cleaner until Julius approves them! I expect he thinks they'll pick the locks on the filing cabinets unless he intimidates them first.'

'Is he intimidating?' Another bad prospect! She'd thought she might be able to manage Dennis without having to reveal the fact that she would be working every spare minute at building up her own business. But Julius whoever-he-was didn't sound like a good thing at all. The mental picture she got was of a man in his mid-forties, like Dennis, only more aggressive and bad-tempered.

'Yes and no,' Jacquie was saying. 'I was terrified of him at first—all that dynamic energy simmering away. He takes work very seriously, and when you cross him—zap! You're seeing stars for days—the kind that swim before your eyes in a sickening haze, not the romantic ones he probably shows his fiancée——'

His *fiancée*? 'How old is he?' Maybe she'd got the image wrong.

Jacquie shrugged. 'About thirty-three, thirty-four—tall, dark and gorgeous! Zoe cried for days when he got engaged, but she had to admit in the end that Fiona *is* very eligible.'

Not what she'd been expecting, but the type was all too predictable! 'And I suppose he thinks he's God's gift to women?'

'Well, he is!' Jacquie said earnestly, her round eyes goggling a little. 'Although he doesn't seem to notice women much—as women, if you know what I mean. Not the ones who work for him, anyway. He's got a huge house in Wiltshire as well as a cottage in one of the villages round here. I know the Prior Harding offices don't look like very much, but he and Dennis are absolutely coining it! They keep costs down by staying out of London, and Julius seems to have a sixth sense when it comes to the investments. I sometimes wonder if he won't be arrested for insider dealing one of these days.'

So Julius was the 'Prior' part of the company. 'You mean he's crooked?'

'Heavens no! I was only joking.' Jacquie sounded horrified.

'So I've only got to see him because the cleaners do?'

'Not exactly. In your case——'

But she wasn't destined to find out her case at that precise moment because Zoe, the other secretary she had met earlier and recognised instantly because of her startling ginger hair, burst into the tea rooms and dived towards their table.

'He's back,' she announced breathlessly, 'and he wants you at the office *this minute*! He's got to go out again before half-past four.'

'I'll pay the bill,' Jacquie said, with bustling efficiency. She was already on her feet, one arm through the sleeve of her raincoat while the other groped automatically for her purse. 'You get back there, Zo, and take Amy with you. I'll catch you up.'

Amy, taken aback by the air of panic that had suddenly been injected into the quiet tea shop, found her nervous qualm unexpectedly subsiding into a feeling of mild disgust—really, the way they were behaving, you'd think it was a royal audience! Just who did Julius Prior imagine he was? Clutching her own raincoat, she looked around with irritation for her umbrella.

'Come *on*!' Zoe was halfway out of the door.

Yes, sir, no, sir, three bags full, sir! She didn't even have time to get her coat on or put the umbrella up as she panted along the pavement behind the flying Zoe. 'Do I salute when I meet him?'

'What?' Zoe didn't wait to catch her reply, and, well ahead of her, disappeared through the attractive pillars flanking the front door of the Georgian house which had been converted into the offices of Prior Harding Investments.

Thoroughly annoyed, Amy instantly slowed to a walk. Her independent spirit resisted anything that resembled petty dictatorship. It seemed ridiculous to be sprinting along the quiet little streets like that all because some latter-day Hitler couldn't wait two minutes—after he'd kept her hanging about for the best part of an hour! And it wasn't as though she didn't have anything better to do with her time.

She abandoned the idea of struggling into her raincoat—there wasn't much point now—but she put her umbrella up. There was still no sign of Jacquie.

Then, as she reached the front steps, the slim heel of the only suitable pair of shoes she possessed stuck between the uneven flagstones, and with an unexpected wrench she found herself hopping forwards at a surprising speed, while the shoe remained wedged in the pavement. She hopped back again to pick it up, and the heel came off in her hand...

With heroic self-control she resisted two overwhelming impulses at once—to shout the worst swear word she could think of at the top of her voice, and to hurl the offending shoe at the nearest litter-bin. With such a vital interview ahead of her, this had better not be an omen...

Jacquie panted up to her elbow.

'Oh, bad luck—come upstairs and I'll see if I can find something to stick it with—I'm sure there's some Superglue in the desk.'

Amy tried to quell her rising exasperation with life—destiny—the entire universe, to ask calmly, 'But what about my interview with the Führer?'

'Who?'

'Mr Prior—Julius—whatever you call him.'

But Jacquie was already shepherding her through the step-ladders and paint cans in the hall, and up the flight of stairs that led to the first-floor offices. In order to negotiate them with any degree of safety she had to take the other shoe off, and that was awkward because there was a huge crescent of red nail varnish round the hole in the toe of her tights. Usually careless of her appearance, she'd made a special effort to look smart and efficient for this interview—but what was the point, she asked herself in exasperation, when fate intended all along to defeat you?

And fate was still at it, if what happened next was anything to go by. As she reached the open reception area at the top of the stairs, Jacquie behind her, a door flew open and a dark-haired man strode through it.

'Zoe! Where's that bloody Thompson woman? I thought I told you to go and fetch her! I've got exactly ten minutes—I'm not taking her on without——'

And then he came to an abrupt halt.

Amy in her turn faltered to a standstill.

It just had to be...

He was quite tall, but not unusually so; quite good-looking, but again not startlingly. But there definitely *was* something about him that could stop you dead in your tracks... With undisguised interest she examined the rather long face, with its straight nose and cleft chin and firmly drawn mouth, while he seemed to be taking in, very slowly, everything from her bedraggled hair downwards—damp jacket, rather short skirt, rather long mud-splashed legs, and last but definitely not least—the scarlet-ringed hole in one stocking.

Then his eyes met hers. He had the most unusual eyes—long fine dark lashes shadowed them, and they were a clear, lucent grey, grey like the sea, the irises ringed with darker colour. Eyes that were unexpectedly thoughtful while they gave nothing away.

Then she was aware that the voice that had been shouting only seconds before was saying quite pleasantly, 'Have you hurt your foot?'

But the merest sea-change in those disquieting eyes just before he spoke warned her to be wary: in that moment he seemed to have come to some decision about her. She was very much afraid it wasn't in her favour. If she wanted this job she really was going to have to fight for it—and letting herself be put at a disadvantage by an unfortunate moment of introduction wasn't the way to go about it. She guessed that if Julius Prior could be impressed by anyone it wasn't going to be an inept weed who let life's little accidents get the better of her!

'Yes!' she said, with the lightest edge of defiance. 'Tropical Sunset' by no stretch of the imagination could be described as blood-colour.

His eyes flicked over her again briefly. 'And do you usually carry your raincoat about like that on wet days?' There was just a hint of amused criticism now.

'I didn't have time to put it on.' He was taller than her, and that mildness in his tone was deceptive: she could sense a sort of leashed energy in him that could be very intimidating if she let it. And then she remembered she wasn't the only one in a potentially embarrassing situation and that little demon of defiance pushed her a step further.

She had a particular curving smile, a smile she'd often been told was fascinatingly enigmatic and witch-like. She tried it now on Julius Prior as she announced in her sweetest, quietest voice, '*I'm* that bloody Thompson woman.'

There was an audible gasp from Jacquie behind her, but she couldn't read the slight change in expression on the face of the dark-haired man. Then he crossed the passage at a stride and held out his hand. 'I'm Julius Prior——' But she'd known that from the moment she saw him.

In the hand she needed to shake his, she found herself clutching her shoes, and she passed them—in three pieces—to Jacquie. Then, because the shoes had been muddy and she had dirt on her fingers, she automatically wiped them on her skirt as though it had been her usual apron, before she offered her hand. It didn't occur to her that she had done anything odd until she saw the look—fully legible this time—on Julius's face as the dark eyebrows shot up in amazement.

The ensuing silence became electric, and then he said, 'You'd better come into my office, Am—er—Miss Thompson. Jacquie—take Miss Thompson's shoes down to that heel bar in the High Street, would you? Tell them it's urgent and then come straight back here. I'll drop her off to collect them when I leave for Oxford. Miss Thompson?'

She followed him, closing the office door behind her. He hadn't even waited politely like Dennis for her to go in first. Perhaps she'd gone a bit too far with that last remark. But he hadn't asked her to leave. Yet.

She could feel the adrenalin pumping through her blood, and took a deep careful breath to slow a nervously rapid heartbeat. Now. This was what it was all about. The next few minutes would decide what sort of a future she and Charlie were going to get.

Julius Prior picked up a sheet of typed paper from the desk, a handwritten letter stapled to the top of it. She recognised it instantly as her own c.v. and letter of application. Then he turned to face her, and propped himself against the desk, arms folded, long legs stretched out in front of him, one ankle casually crossed over the other. He had lean thighs and slim hips, and the charcoal-grey business suit he was wearing looked as though it had been measured to fit by a very expensive tailor.

The lucid grey eyes again regarded her thoughtfully. Refusing to let him daunt her, she returned the stare and wondered if he'd even ask her to sit down. Involuntarily, she curled her toes into the heavy-duty carpet.

'Red hair and blue eyes,' he said at last. 'And what would an Irish witch with limited relevant experience—and a curious choice of referees—be doing applying to work in an office like this?'

Her heart sank. Not a very auspicious opening! He obviously thought her a long way short of the requirements.

'I applied for the post because I was sure I could handle it.' She was amazed at how cool she managed to sound. She knew what that remark about references was alluding to, but couldn't bring herself to explain it. Not just yet. 'I know it doesn't look as though I've had a very consistent career as a secretary, but it does mean I've got *varied* experience,' she persuaded.

'Y-e-s.' The slow, thoughtful drawl wasn't exactly encouraging, and that sea colour of his eyes was suspiciously steely now. 'We can't afford to "nanny" anyone in this job, Miss Thompson. You sink or swim from day one. There's another thing—we won't even consider anyone who isn't prepared to commit herself fully, which means if you're asked to work late you work late, and if you're asked to come in early you come in early. That's why we pay such high salaries. The last secretary who had the post found she couldn't give the job that sort of commitment. We can't take on anyone who has half her mind on home problems. Do you have home problems, Miss Thompson?'

The question was fired at her in a manner calculated to disconcert, but she had seen it coming.

'No,' she lied. There was no way he could check. He gestured to a chair—that was hopeful. She sat down with some relief, but there was no break in the inquisition.

'When exactly did you do your secretarial training? I'm a little unclear as to the dates in all this.'

As she had meant him to be. She'd left them out. With the careful way she'd presented all the information, Dennis Harding hadn't noticed. Trust the famous Julius to have seen the flaws! There had been an unpleasant edge to that last remark.

'When I left school.'

'And how long was the course?'

She'd have to tell the truth this time. She knew instinctively that this man wouldn't give her one more second of his time if he could actually catch her out. It was a pity she'd had to see him at all. She was sure now that Dennis would have given her at least a couple of months' trial. 'Twelve weeks,' she admitted, and met his look squarely.

'Twelve *weeks*? You learned shorthand in twelve weeks?'

'Speedwriting and typing. None of my former employers seemed to find it inadequate.'

Julius appeared to consider the flash of slanting blue eyes that accompanied that remark, but it didn't deflect the course of his interrogation. 'Your former employers—you didn't work for any of them for long, except Matlock and West?'

The need to earn a regular salary hadn't been something she'd had to worry about in those days, and she'd taken a series of part-time secretarial jobs merely to fill in the gaps, when the money wasn't coming in from the business she was trying to start up herself. She hadn't even bothered to mention on the c.v. some of the jobs she'd done. The true extent of her patchy background wouldn't recommend her to anyone wanting a seriously committed full-time secretary, and she didn't think it wise to give any hint that her real qualifications were in the catering business—because that, of course, was where her commitment still lay.

At that moment there was a knock at the door, and before Julius had time to make a reply Zoe put her head round.

'The coffee you asked for earlier, Mr Prior—shall I bring it in?'

He nodded curtly in her direction, and, as though the interruption signalled a change into another gear, shot one immaculately white shirt-cuff up his wrist, and glanced impatiently at the heavy gold watch he was wearing.

There was a brief silence while Julius Prior watched Amy, and Amy watched Zoe as she went to the huge antique desk against which her boss had propped himself. She put down a tray set with two cups and a sugar bowl. Then Amy's eyes followed her retreat as she shut the office door behind her, only too well aware that the disconcerting Mr Prior was still scrutinising *her*.

'So you haven't worked for anyone very long?' he prompted.

'Not really,' she said carefully. 'I moved around quite a bit—but not because I didn't like the jobs. I'm sure any of those firms I've listed would give me a reference.'

'But why, when your most recent long spell of employment was for Matlock and West, didn't you ask them for a reference?'

'The company folded about five months ago.'

'You couldn't have written to any of your former bosses?'

'My former boss was my father. Matlock and West was his company.'

'And you didn't want to ask him?' The question was only marginally less aggressive.

Amy, her face impassive after months of practice, deliberately relaxed the toes that were curled into the carpet, and then said, 'My father—both my parents— were killed earlier this year in a flying accident.'

She was aware that Julius Prior had glanced swiftly at her c.v. again, and was looking at her, though she refused to meet his gaze directly. 'I'm sorry,' he said briefly. And then, as though her bereaved state merited some special treatment—or merely prompted him to remember his manners—he said, 'Would you like a cup of coffee?'

He held out the cup to her, and then offered the sugar bowl.

Remembering Jacquie's reaction to her sugar consumption, and unwilling to draw Julius's attention to herself as any more of an oddity—he had already found quite enough to comment on in her general appearance—she limited herself to one unremarkable spoonful, and hoped she wouldn't be obliged to drink the whole cup.

The social interlude now appeared to be over, because he instantly switched back into business mode, glancing down at her letter again. There was a sceptical, downward turn to the corners of that firm mouth. 'So what it amounts to, Miss Thompson, is that you've only once been in full-time secretarial employment of this sort, and that was for about three months when you were working for your father. Otherwise it's only been occasional temping. Am I right?'

He sounded so patently unimpressed that her heart sank even lower—there wasn't much chance he'd offer her the job now.

'Well, sort of. But...'

He didn't wait for her to finish. 'What prompted you to apply for this particular post?'

He'd already asked her that. What was he trying to do, catch her out changing her story?

People like Julius Prior thought they ruled the world. They could ask any questions they chose, and because she wanted the job she was obliged to answer. And the answer was boringly obvious. She began to feel very hostile.

'I needed to earn money—like most people!'

If she'd expected a reaction, she was disappointed. 'Do you think you can cope with pressure?'

If I couldn't cope with pressure I wouldn't be here now... She looked him dead in the eyes, and in her own there was a sudden determined glint.

'Try me,' she said.

He was silent for a moment, his eyes holding hers, assessing her again. Her crossed fingers tightened in her lap and she found that she was holding her breath. I don't like you very much, and you probably don't like me, but please, please just give me a chance!

He had given no clues at all as to what he really thought of her.

Then, just as she was certain he was about to show her the door, he said, 'All right. You can have two months to prove to me you can do the job. You start tomorrow.'

Tomorrow.

There was another silence, Amy's this time.

'Tomorrow?'

The dark brows drew together in a quick frown. 'Doesn't that suit you? Your letter stated you'd be ready to start any time. It's important we have someone to fill the position as soon as possible.'

She saw him glance at his watch again, as though the word 'time' instantly had him on the hop. Her own mind began to race—she couldn't afford to antagonise him now, but how on earth was she going to find a spare minute to do all that food shopping for tomorrow night's dinner booking? She couldn't go to the late-night supermarket because she'd have to be serving for tonight's booking while it was open. After the interview, perhaps?

'Miss Thompson?'

There was no question of negotiating—he'd change his mind about employing her. She repressed an impatient sigh, and met his eyes. What could she see in them—a sudden doubt? Criticism? She asked quickly, 'What time would you like me to get in?'

'Eight-thirty?'

He'd made the point about working flexible hours fairly forcibly. She hoped none of her dismay showed in her face.

'We've got a board meeting at nine,' he said curtly. 'I'd like you to be here early to help check everything. Zoe will get the boardroom ready tonight.' He stood up abruptly. 'I have to be going in about three minutes. I'll give you a lift to the heel bar—you shouldn't have to wait long for your shoes. Where's your raincoat?'

'Zoe took it for me—Mr Prior?'

He was the one to look surprised now. Almost as though, she thought, having made a quick decision about her and given the instructions he considered relevant, he'd mentally filed her away until tomorrow.

'Yes?'

'Am I working for Mr Harding or for you?' She let just the tiniest hint of criticism creep into her voice. 'I thought the advertisement was for a secretary to Mr Harding.' Purely as a physical specimen, Julius Prior might be very attractive, but she was certain she'd have one hell of a time if he was the one to give her the orders. It wasn't at all easy to see why the other two secretaries actually liked him. If she could establish from the beginning that she was the more easygoing Dennis's property, then he mightn't cross her path too often.

'Officially you will be Mr Harding's secretary—Zoe! Get Miss Thompson's coat, will you ... ?'

And that 'officially' was all the information she was destined to get, because the next moment he was picking up his own cup of coffee to consume it in three gulps, and pulling a face afterwards. Then the ginger-haired secretary was back again carrying Amy's raincoat, a shoe, and two umbrellas.

'Jacquie only took one of Miss Thompson's shoes,' she explained. 'She's in Mr Harding's office now if you want to see her.'

'No need,' said Julius Prior briskly, with a glance at Amy as she put her own lukewarm coffee, virtually untasted, back on the tray. She had no intention of choking over it and then having to set off at a run. He was already by the door.

'Oh, and Zoe——'

'Yes, Mr Prior?'

'Get out your dictionary when we've gone, will you, and have a good long look at the definition of "hot"?'

Ouch! thought Amy. Rather than paths not crossing too often, I hope they don't cross at all! But when she looked at Zoe to see how she was taking it she was amazed to find her grinning. She glanced quickly at her new employer—or rather, since she was keen to split hairs in this particular case, her new employer's co-director.

There wasn't the ghost of a smile on his face. Then he caught her look and she saw quite clearly the sparkle in those sea-grey eyes.

It wasn't what she'd expected at all.

There was scarcely time for a hurried goodbye to Zoe before she was on her way downstairs in Julius's wake. They negotiated the paint tins and step-ladders at speed and then she nearly ran into his back as he came to an unexpected halt in the doorway. He half turned to look back at her, and then glanced down at her stockinged feet.

'Wait here,' he instructed. 'I'll bring the car round. You can't hop about the street like that.' She was surprised he had remembered. 'Will you want a lift across the pavement?'

The antagonism, or whatever it had been, of the interview had mysteriously melted away. She caught his eye. Again there was that gleam she had seen when he'd chastised Zoe for the condition of the coffee. She gave him a sideways glance, remembering a comment he'd made about her, and took a risk. 'We witches have our ways of getting about,' she said demurely. 'Aren't you afraid I might put a spell on you?'

It was a relief after the earlier tension to hear him laugh. It sounded like genuine amusement.

'For all I know you might have done that already! Where did you leave the broomstick?'

'At home with the cat. It tends to stall a bit in the rain. Charlie says it needs servicing, but the local garage only specialises in Volkswagens.'

His eyes narrowed a fraction. 'Who's Charlie?'

She never knew afterwards why she'd said it. After all, there was no reason in the world not to tell him Charlie was her brother—except that family commitments, especially problematic ones, were a bad idea. 'The person I live with,' she said ambiguously.

One dark eyebrow twitched fractionally upwards, and then he was striding out into the rain, automatic umbrella instantly unfurling itself against the heavy patter of drops.

The car that appeared at the end of the street after a couple of minutes was a discreet grey Mercedes, for size not ideal in the streets of a small Oxfordshire market town, Amy reflected idly, having wondered what sort of flashy sports model the eligible Mr Prior would drive.

Then the Mercedes pulled up in front of her and the passenger door opened. She could see him leaning across the passenger seat. 'Come on—let's see this witchy way of getting across wet pavements, then!'

She slipped on her one shoe, and hopped quickly out into the rain, manoeuvring carefully so that she could sit in the passenger seat without letting her other foot touch the ground. Then she pulled the door shut and looked at him, breathing rather fast, her cheeks slightly flushed. Unexpectedly, he was grinning.

'I'm disappointed! I expected you to float across on a boat made out of a wet leaf or dry up the street in a blast of magic. What happened? Leave the spell book at home?'

And just what had happened to that intimidating time-is-money tycoon? she wondered. Julius Prior was turning out to have a nicer side to him than she'd thought. It wasn't like her to feel so prickly about anyone on first meeting. It must have been her desperation over the job. Well, he'd given it to her. The rest was up to her now.

They were already gliding comfortably down the street, and the unexpected luxury of it struck Amy forcefully. It seemed a long time ago—another life—when she'd been able to take for granted such luxuries herself.

'The best witches don't waste their power on minor matters like crossing the road,' she said, merely making conversation now. 'They save it up for something really special. And by the way, I'm not Irish.'

They were drawing up in front of a small hardware store, its plate-glass windows displaying an uninteresting clutter of spanners, plastic buckets, lengths of hose, mortice locks and jugs. One sign said 'Keys cut' and another 'Heel Bar'.

He turned sideways to her, one arm draped over the steering-wheel, the other along the back of the seat.

'Forgive me if I don't wait to see if your shoe's all right,' he said. 'I've got another appointment.'

She turned to him politely. 'You've been very kind. I hope this isn't going to make you late.'

The formality seemed rather false after the high-tension exchanges earlier in the office, and the other extreme of the broomstick jokes that had followed. But then he smiled, a real smile this time that took her by surprise—and suddenly she saw exactly what had made Zoe cry for days at the news of his engagement.

'Not at all. It isn't every day I interview a witch—certainly not with hair the colour of red seaweed. I look forward to a tea-leaf consultation some time, Miss Thompson! See you tomorrow.'

She wasn't aware of getting out of the car, or shutting the door, but she supposed she must have done both because she found herself standing on one foot in the middle of the pavement watching the grey car glide away into the rain, tyres sending up a fine spray from the wet road.

Red seaweed! Was that supposed to be a *compliment*?

Well . . . She'd got a job that was going to pay the rent money—for as long as she could juggle two different careers. She and Charlie and the cat weren't going to starve yet awhile, or find themselves living in cardboard boxes, or busking in shopping centres on Saturdays—at least she and the cat weren't.

What else had she achieved on this most inauspicious of days? Well, she'd met her boss, and liked him, and she'd met the other secretaries and liked them. And she'd met her boss's partner. But she wasn't sure what she felt about the soon-to-be-married Mr Prior. 'Liking' somehow didn't seem a very relevant word for whatever it was.

She'd better go inside and find out what had happened to her shoe.

CHAPTER TWO

'CHARLIE, get up!' she said firmly.

There was a groan and a heave and the only visible portion of her brother—a few stiffened spikes of carroty hair—disappeared under the pillow.

'Too early.' The mumble was almost unintelligible. Mercilessly she twitched back the duvet, exposing exactly half of him to the chill November morning with the accuracy of a couple of months' practice.

'I want to see you out of bed and dressed before I leave—I told you last night I had to catch the seven-thirty bus and if I miss it because of you it'll be a bed full of ice cubes tomorrow morning—and that's a promise!' A contorted movement, and one light blue eye glared at her balefully. The other was squeezed tightly shut.

'I might get up if you hadn't taken the fire,' was the resentful reply, scarcely more articulate than the first.

Amy sighed. She felt mean, but what else could she do? Charlie was so forgetful.

'What can you expect if you leave it on all day when we're both out? Apart from the fact that you could burn the cat to a cinder—not to mention the house—I can't afford the electricity bills. *Five* minutes, Charlie and then it's the cold-water treatment! I'm not losing this job before I've even started.'

Every morning is a battle, she thought tiredly. I'm like a limp rag before the day even gets going! But she couldn't blame him; what fourteen-year-old ever wanted to crawl out of bed with only the prospect of getting himself to school on a rainy day to lure him?

Since the deaths of their parents in the spring, she'd become increasingly aware of her responsibility for her young brother. With their sex and age-difference—there was an eight-year gap—there could be no rivalry between them. They'd always had a good relationship, but now, lacking the authority of a parent, she was finding it more and more difficult to cope with him. He usually gave in after an argument, and she tried to keep those to the real essentials, but she couldn't *force* him to do anything. They'd never fought physically, but being able to pick him up and dump him in the bath, as her mother had done when he was little, was an easy solution no longer open to her. Charlie was thin, like her, but his adolescent strength was more than a match for hers, as she'd discovered from their occasional teasing bouts. He might be her little brother in every other way but that didn't mean she could treat him as a child.

The trauma of the accident had drawn them together, briefly, with a closeness they'd never had before. After his initial reaction of shocked disbelief, Charlie had at first withdrawn into himself. She suspected that he had been pressured by the role he felt obliged to play, as support to his sister. He had considered himself too old to cry like the boy he still was, and Amy herself, only just beginning to be aware of the problems of debt that faced them, hadn't yet been able to come to terms with the full extent of the changes to their lives.

Then one night he had crept into her room as he had done when he was very young, giving in at last to his secret grief, and they had both cried until they had no more tears left. Neither had alluded to the incident afterwards, Amy chiefly because she guessed Charlie was walking a particularly precarious inner tightrope, and needed to believe he could cope without showing childish weakness. She hoped she would be there for him if he needed her, but he was making her feel increasingly inadequate. Most of the time she could do little but leave what appeared to be well enough alone.

Rasputin, a fat-faced tabby, wound himself round her ankles lovingly as she stood by the fridge, cereal bowl in one hand and felt-tip pen in the other.

'Go away,' she said, her mouth full of muesli, 'you've been fed.'

Celery.

Walnuts.

Whipping cream.

Yet more butter.

The list was going to be endless. She'd have to ring Jess from the office to remind her to get the fish—and did they have any almonds? If she'd had time to contact her last night it would have made things easier, but the party she'd been catering for had gone on too late. She picked her way across the kitchen floor between piles of dishes—she'd been too tired to do them before she went to bed—and examined the contents of the store cupboard. No almonds. Back to the list.

There was an offended yowl from the cat.

'Hell's bells, Rasputin! Can't you look where you leave your tail? *Charlie*! One more minute and I'll be up with the wet sponge!' What was it she was going to write down? Oh, yes, almonds...and cling film. She'd used the last of the roll on the quiches for the Horticultural Society—she must remember to ring Jess about those too.

She felt quite irritated that the bus was late, having made it to the stop against all the odds with one minute still to spare. Luckily it wouldn't matter much at the other end, since she'd have nearly half an hour to kill before she could get into the offices in Wychford. Half an hour in the rain again.

Tomorrow, hopefully, would be a whole lot better. The timing with the buses would be more convenient and she wouldn't have such a battle with Rip van Winkle—well, she would, but she needn't feel so cruel about it. If she could just get through today without making a mess of it!

She'd liked the bespectacled Dennis, and Jacquie and Zoe had seemed friendly and helpful. In fact, there was only one fly in what could turn out to be some very acceptable ointment—Julius Prior. What a pity he had to be the one with all the power! But with any luck he might be out of the office seeing clients most of the time.

She had no idea why she felt so strongly about him. After all, he had given her the job. But somehow he seemed to pose a threat to her and she wasn't sure why. He could fire her, yes, and he was going to be far more exacting than Dennis if she had to do any work for him, but that didn't seem to account for it entirely. That uneasy mixture of business drive and humour had something to do with it, but she wasn't sure what. Maybe it was simply that it was a bit unnerving to find herself working for a man who could be so obviously attractive, and was at the same time so very unavailable. Jacquie had said he didn't notice other women, but that wasn't entirely the impression she'd got.

Once off the bus in Wychford, she made her way slowly to the offices. There was no point hanging about in the drizzling rain. The shops, such as they were, weren't open yet, and she might as well let the inconsiderate Mr Prior know that not only was she at the office on time, but that *he'd* kept *her* waiting. It was only just past eight o'clock.

But to her surprise she'd hardly reached the doorstep before she recognised the tall figure striding up from the end of the street, raincoat flapping, briefcase in one hand and umbrella in the other.

'Miss Thompson! I did say eight-thirty—or is this a "first morning" bid to impress the management?'

'I hadn't much choice,' she said shortly. 'The only bus I could get leaves my village at half-past seven.' With a quick scattering of raindrops he shook the umbrella, collapsed it and handed it to her, almost, she thought, as though her sole purpose were to be standing there ready to take it from him! Then he fished in his pocket for the bunch of keys that unlocked the offices. She found herself looking at that cleft in his chin.

'You don't have a car?'

'Well, I do, but it's got something wrong with the engine at the moment.'

'Can you trust your garage?'

'Oh, yes.' She could smell just the faintest whiff of aftershave and clean masculine soap on the sharp morning air, and wondered if his fiancée lived with him, and what it was like to be kissed goodbye by him in the mornings. She followed him into the hall, still carrying his umbrella. He seemed to have forgotten about it, unless that was part of her job too—to carry his things like a lackey. She half expected to be handed his briefcase as well.

'Mind the paint tins. A good local mechanic is worth his weight in gold. Is yours in the village?'

'Er—yes.'

There was no garage in Applecot, but it wouldn't have made any difference even if there had been. She couldn't possibly afford to have the car seen to. It had been parked off the road in a neighbour's drive for the past four months. Maybe, when she'd fed a few salary cheques into her starving bank account, she'd have it looked at. Or if, by some wonderful chance, she and Jess got a

couple of really lucrative weekend parties to cook for...
But then there was the question of the road tax.

Once they were upstairs, Julius didn't waste time, and
issued a flood of instructions before either of them had
got their coats off. Since cooking for parties was one
long, juggling act, Amy automatically sorted the tasks
into a table of priorities and had the coffee on before
she started in the boardroom. Zoe, it appeared, had got
through only half the required preparations the night
before.

'There was a last-minute crisis which involved a couple
of letters to type after Jacquie had gone, so Dennis told
me on the phone last night,' he explained.

Amy had the feeling that the information wasn't given
to her merely out of interest—he was letting her know
that sloping off with tasks incomplete was only tolerated
in exceptional circumstances. It also gave the impression
that business went on virtually twenty-four hours a day.

She was halfway through doling out directors' reports
round the table in the small boardroom when the phone
rang. She could see through the open door that Julius
was standing right next to it.

'Answer that, will you?' He gave a curt nod in the
direction of the phone. He was frowning at the desk diary
in his hand and even moved away from the shrill
summons to stand at the window, his back to her.

Amy was taken aback. It wouldn't have hurt him just
to pick it up! Maybe this was a test? See how many jobs
you can do at once, Miss Thompson! Score above average—anything over ten, shall we say?—and we'll keep
you on for the week!

Resisting the temptation to deal the remaining folders
carelessly across the table like a deck of cards, she hurried
to the phone. 'Prior Harding Investments—can I
help you?'

There was no time to ask or explain anything, because the caller was clearly used to rapid dictating over the phone, and after a peremptory, 'Take this down...' she found herself scribbling incomprehensibly on the nearest piece of paper. He could have been talking Ancient Greek for all the sense she could make of the information coming across the line—something about a take-over and diluting the stocks and something else about a rights issue—or was it rites? Or even possibly writes? And then, 'Let Julius know when he gets in, will you?' She looked across helplessly at the man in question to find him watching her, the desk diary still open in his hands, and an unreadable look on his face.

'Do you want to speak to——?' she began into the phone, and then the unreadable look became all too legible.

A fierce frown drew the dark eyebrows together and he mouthed an unmistakable, 'No!'

'Er—I'll tell him as soon as he arrives——' she said into the mouthpiece, and then the line went dead. Whoever it was didn't believe in hanging about.

'Why the hell did you think I wanted you to answer the phone?' he demanded. 'Don't ever tell anyone I'm here before you've asked me!'

She digested that. He crossed back to the desk. 'Was it Bill Mortimer?'

'I didn't have time to find out—he——'

'You have worked in an office before, Miss Thompson?'

It was just the tone he'd used telling Zoe to look up 'hot' in the dictionary the previous day, but this time his eyes were anything but amused. She knew then that her first impressions of him had been right: Julius Prior was going to be perfectly bloody to work for. Her own eyes flashed a sudden dangerous blue, and she said with acid sweetness, 'Never with people who speak like machines!' And turned on her heel.

'Miss Thompson.'

She hadn't even got to the boardroom door. Keeping a tight hold of her temper, and arranging her most consciously bewitching smile, she turned back. His tone warned her that it hadn't been the wisest remark she'd ever made, given the circumstances. The best thing to do would be to apologise, even if she didn't mean it.

The expression changed on his face as she looked at him—it hadn't exactly been anger she glimpsed, but the harder lines visibly softened.

'Look,' he said, 'even if it is your first morning and I can't afford to have you walk out before we've even started, I did warn you there wasn't time for holding anybody's hand in this company.'

She said guardedly, 'I don't want anybody to hold my hand, thank you.'

One dark eyebrow quirked slightly. 'What a pity,' he said. 'That's rather a waste.'

The sudden change of meaning was disconcerting. It wasn't what she'd been led to expect by Jacquie—veiled reprimand one minute and sexual innuendo the next. She didn't like the flirtatious tone, not from him anyway. It seemed dishonest, but she didn't stop to analyse further.

'Would your fiancée like you making that sort of remark?' she asked pointedly. She might as well let him see straight away that she knew what the score was. For a moment he looked surprised, and displeased.

'Gossiping already, Miss Thompson?'

'It wasn't the kind of information I asked for, no.'

There was a loaded silence while he looked at her and she returned the stare. She was getting off to a very bad start; could you sack someone merely on incompatibility grounds? At the rate she was going, she wouldn't even get the chance to walk out first. She lowered her eyes, unwilling to meet the look in his any longer. Then she said, with deliberate meekness, 'Shall I get back to those directors' reports?'

'Any chance of coffee before you do?'

It wasn't the reply she expected, but she felt an instant sense of relief. It signalled that he wasn't going to give her her marching orders yet!

I'm not cut out for this sort of job, she thought. I don't like being at someone's beck and call, and I'd much rather be working for myself, whatever the problems. Roll on the day Jess and I open our own restaurant!

Coffee... If she didn't have something hot and sweet to drink soon, she'd die! She thought regretfully of the half-eaten bowl of muesli still on top of the fridge. She'd never had time to finish it.

Julius followed her to the cubby-hole that passed as a kitchen; equipped with fridge, a small microwave and an electric kettle, it could cope with anything from iced drinks for the unexpected guest to hot lunches for the directors in times of crisis. She was conscious of him standing in the doorway, and wished he'd go away. She could feel him behind her, as though he were some sort of magnet and she were covered with a lot of little steel prickles that instantly bristled in his direction. It was a weird sensation.

The percolator had finished fizzing to itself and she poured out two cups, and then looked at him with just the merest hint of a challenge.

'I am allowed to have some, aren't I?'

'Of course. What time did you have breakfast if you had to catch a seven o'clock bus?'

'Oh, not too early,' she said dismissively. She wasn't going to mention the fact that 'breakfast' had been more of an idea than an actuality. 'Milk?'

'Please. No sugar.'

Her hand touched his as she passed him his cup, and his own drew back involuntarily, almost as though she'd given him a tiny electric shock. She stared at him in surprise, her slanting blue eyes wide.

'You're frozen!' he exclaimed. 'Why don't you put some more clothes on?'

She shrugged. 'Oh, I'm always cold in the winter. And we don't have central heating at home. I warmed up a bit on the bus, but it's faded now. Don't the radiators work in this building?'

'They're programmed to come on at about nine. Are you sure you're all right? I don't want you fainting from hypothermia or anything—especially not today. There's too much going on.' She felt uncomfortable under his critical gaze. 'You're too thin. You should eat more.'

'That's what Jacquie said yesterday, and I assured her I eat like a horse.' When I get time, she added mentally.

He watched her, fascinated as Jacquie had been by the way she spooned the customary sugar into her cup.

'Do you usually drink it like that?'

'Energy,' she said succinctly. This was getting to be a replay of her trip to the Wistaria Tea Rooms, except that she'd quite enjoyed talking to Jacquie. She wished Julius would go away and get on with whatever it was he'd come in early to do. She couldn't get rid of the impression that he was just waiting for her to make another mistake.

Once the other two secretaries had turned up—on the dot of nine o'clock—she felt more secure. Her hour with Julius had put her straight in the firing line. At least she could shelter behind them now. One small point in Julius's favour, though—he had turned on the heating early. Perhaps he had felt the cold too?

It didn't take long to discover that gossip was the life-blood of the office. Jacquie and Zoe took every opportunity to exchange the latest items and share them with

Amy who, with heaps of typing inherited from her pre-
decessor—the one who had walked out—would have appreciated the time to get on with it; she was no expert
typist. But everything, from Dennis's wife phoning because she had to take the dogs to the vet to what Julius
had said to Zoe when she went into his office to take a
letter, was discussed in detail.

And it was the subject of Julius that really got them
going—when, and where, he'd next take his fiancée out
to lunch, what they'd eat, why she hadn't turned up at
all last week, whether they'd had a row... Amy was
convinced by the end of the morning that there was not
much left to find out about the blonde, rich twenty-two-
year-old Fiona Harper-Maxwell, who had only met Julius
a matter of weeks before they'd got engaged. She felt
she knew Mrs Harper-Maxwell intimately too, because
she was organising the wedding. The way Jacquie described it, it sounded like a military campaign.

'She came here once with Fiona,' Zoe confided,
loitering past Amy's desk in the reception area while the
board meeting was in progress. 'She's pretty terrifying—
smiles a lot while her eyes kind of drill through you.
Poor Julius—what a mother-in-law! And Fiona looked
quite sheepish while she was around.'

Lunch was even more of an 'idea' than breakfast had
been as far as Amy was concerned, because although
she got her statutory hour she was forced to spend it
trawling the supermarket for the ingredients for dinner
that evening. Jess worked flexi-time in a bank in Oxford,
and although she was finishing work earlier than Amy
she wouldn't have time to do much shopping if she was
to beat the traffic queues and get to Wychford to pick
up Amy on the dot of five. They usually did most of
the cooking at Jess's, which was more convenient, and
prepared the last-minute stuff on site.

They were definitely cutting things a bit fine for this evening. It was lucky the menu was so simple—it was just the quantities that seemed enormous—or perhaps that was because they were having to stock up on a lot of basics. She eyed the four bulky supermarket bags stacked by her desk in the reception area with some misgiving. There was nowhere else to put them. Apart from the fact that they wouldn't make the best of impressions on any visitor, she didn't want to have to field enquiries as to why she found it necessary to buy so much food at once, especially if it was going to have to be a recurring feature of her days at Prior's. The less any of them knew about her freelance catering business, the better.

It was the middle of the afternoon before she had time to retrieve her sandwiches from her handbag. They were squashed very flat and to save time she decided to eat all three as a sort of triple-decker; the peanut butter and cream cheese were OK together, but the jam wasn't such a good idea.

Typing with one finger, monster sandwich in hand and her mouth full, she looked up with dismay as a figure appeared on the stairs.

Of course, it *had* to be. Not Dennis, whom she'd hardly spoken to all day, but Julius.

He stared at her in silence for a full ten seconds, taking in the supermarket carriers, one of which had keeled over to release a chocolate cake—Charlie's favourite—and a couple of packets of biscuits. Then he said, 'I give you a lunch-hour precisely for the purpose of putting food into your mouth, Amy. What happened to you between one and two o'clock today?'

At that moment Jacquie emerged from Dennis's office carrying a document and went to one of the filing cabinets.

Amy chewed and swallowed quickly. 'I had a lunch-hour,' she said in a tone of careful apology. 'I'm sorry, it's just that——'

He didn't wait for the excuse. 'Then in future could you restrict yourself to the official eating hours? Or, at the very least, use the kitchen? Visiting clients aren't going to be impressed by a secretary who treats the reception area as a cafeteria. Jacquie, will you come into my office for a minute?'

She watched him cross to his office, Jacquie, with a wink at Amy, following him. The door shut behind them. She felt both annoyed and relieved at the same time; she had to admit that he'd had a point, but he didn't have to sound so sarcastic about it! But he hadn't called her Amy before. Could that be a signal of acceptance, despite her transgressions?

He really puzzled her. There seemed to be some curious contradiction in him. 'Yes and no,' Jacquie had said when asked if he was intimidating—and that was about as near as it was possible to get to a description of him. She wondered what he'd be like out of the context of the office and business—did he live his whole life by a stop-watch, never really free of the preoccupations of the wheeling-and-dealing world in which he made his living? That would be a pity. Somehow she got the feeling that there might be a very different man underneath all the high-powered gloss. It was just something about those extraordinary eyes.

Five o'clock couldn't come round fast enough, and as soon as the minute hand of her watch touched the hour she was tidying away at double-quick speed. Luckily there were no letters outstanding, and she couldn't see any reason why anyone should stop her leaving. After all, she'd been there since eight—if Julius had had any decency at all he'd have let her go at least half an hour early.

Just in case of difficulties she asked Dennis, in the process of packing his own briefcase, if she could go.

'Sure you can!' he said cheerfully. 'I hope we haven't worked you too hard on your first day. Find your way round the filing cabinets all right?'

She gave him a grin. 'OK so far, thanks. But I probably won't be the first to discover I've messed up the system!'

He laughed. 'Don't worry. Nobody's going to jump down your throat for it.'

I know one person who might, she thought as she took her leave, but it didn't seem like a good idea to voice her misgivings to his partner.

Jacquie was in the reception area, putting on her coat. She showed a keen interest in the carrier bags.

'Is that *all* food?' she asked incredulously.

Amy laughed. 'I told you I eat a lot!' she joked.

Jacquie's reply sounded wistful. 'I only have to look at a chocolate cake and I put on a stone.'

Remembering her performance with the iced bun the day before, Amy privately suspected that she did more than just gaze distantly at the more tempting bits of confectionery. But she didn't want to discuss her purchases; if she let Jacquie know she was running a catering business, the news would get about.

'I'm sorry—I'm in an awful rush. A friend's giving me a lift home today—see you tomorrow!'

Tossing a new load of fallen items back into one of the carrier bags, she gathered them together, and, laden like a Christmas tree, staggered down to the street as fast as was compatible with personal safety. It wasn't only Jacquie she was keen to get away from—she could do without another encounter with Mr Prior yet awhile, especially when her transport would proclaim in gold lettering a connection with Cookery Unlimited.

Jess was waiting for her, her mini-van parked on double yellow lines outside. She was squinting in the driving mirror while she tied back a mass of dark curly hair with an inadequate red ribbon.

'Thank goodness!' she exclaimed. 'One more minute and there'd have been a traffic warden breathing steamy fury all over my window! Shall we head straight for my place? We don't have to be at the Rentons' until about seven. I got the meringue done last night. Did you manage to buy any cream?'

They exchanged information quickly as Jess turned north off the main Swindon road towards her own small village.

'So how do you feel after your first day?' she demanded after a while.

'Shattered,' Amy said succinctly. 'There's a real slave-driver of a boss and what annoys me is that I'm not even supposed to be working for him, but for his partner Dennis. I hardly saw Dennis all day.'

'What's this slave-driver like?' Jess asked curiously. 'Middle-aged—whip-cracking—military?'

Amy wrinkled her nose and thought for a moment. 'Just what I imagined before I met him. But no—to be perfectly honest, in any other circumstances I'd say he was rather dishy—the classic tallish, darkish and definitely handsome type, with the most incredible eyes, and the kind of business suits that look as though they've been moulded on to him by his own personal tailor. They're all in love with him—well, not Dennis, of course!—and office gossip makes him out to be fabulously rich.'

Her friend gave a low whistle. 'He sounds absolutely gorgeous! So what's wrong with him? Married?'

Amy laughed. 'You're a natural predator, Jess! Don't you ever think about men in any terms other than "sexually available"?'

'And don't you ever think beyond "Will he give me a job or not?"'

'Chance'd be a fine thing!'

But the tone in Amy's voice wasn't entirely light-hearted, and her friend glanced across at her quickly.

'Sorry, Ames. You've had an appallingly tough time since the crash. But you've managed brilliantly. I know I couldn't have coped with all that financial hassle on top of everything else. But don't worry, the old "Un-limited" is going to make our fortunes, and then we'll be able to pay other people to do the work while we go out on the town every night. So go on telling me about this dishy boss—apart from a *teensy* reservation about the slave-driving, I can't see what's wrong with him!'

'From your point of view,' Amy said firmly, 'it's that he's already engaged! But from mine it's that he expects total devotion to Prior Harding Investments during working hours—and he's already made it threateningly clear that "working hours" are infinitely elastic. So apart from a few minor office mishaps, starting off with trying to make him take a totally incomprehensible phone call this morning, I've already offended him by eating my lunch at three o'clock in full view of visitors, even though there weren't any, and by stacking up my shopping beside my desk. But seriously, Jess, I'm going to have to be careful about raiding the supermarkets. I'm beginning to think they suspect I'm a compulsive shop-lifter or something. I got some very funny looks from all of them this afternoon.'

That was bad news, because they had a big booking for the following night and Jess wasn't going to be able to get time off to shop.

'Don't worry, I'll do it,' said Amy bravely. 'It's none of Mr Julius Prior's business if I spend every lunch-hour of the week in the supermarket!'

Jess looked concerned. 'But if he doesn't like the idea of you doing any other work... If he knew your cir-cumstances, surely——'

'No, Jess!' Amy surprised herself with her own vehemence. It was odd, because the fact that he had made it clear that he didn't want an employee with other commitments didn't seem to have anything to do with it. She wouldn't have felt so strongly about Dennis knowing of her difficulties, even though he didn't want a secretary with home problems either. But, for some reason she was unwilling to analyse, she reacted violently to the suggestion that she should contemplate any overlap between her private world and her work as far as Julius Prior was concerned.

'My personal life has nothing to do with my employer, nor his with me . . .'

CHAPTER THREE

BUT a glimpse into Julius's private world came sooner than Amy had expected. The very next morning a tall, green-eyed blonde walked into the office. Her clothes were unremarkable—jeans and a hand-knitted sweater with a multicoloured design all over it—but there was something about her that suggested money and confidence. Her thick short hair was expensively cut, and apart from the flattering tan, which was obviously genuine, her looks were further enhanced by art, her eyes carefully made up and her lips glossy with a fashionable shade of lipstick.

Most significant of all, she was wearing a large diamond on the third finger of her left hand.

The expression on her face, at first glance, was not encouraging, but then she smiled at Amy, and said quickly, 'Has Julius got someone with him?'

Although they hadn't met before, Fiona Harper-Maxwell clearly assumed that anyone in Julius's employ would know who she was, and that she had automatic right of access.

Amy, feeling unaccountably prickly all of a sudden, gave her receptionist's smile. 'Who shall I say wants him?'

The other woman gave her a sharp look. 'Don't bother,' she said dismissively, and went towards Julius's office. Amy couldn't help speculating on what sort of reception Fiona would have got if he had had someone in there—or perhaps, because she was his fiancée, the rules didn't apply to her?

Zoe, who was lingering by the filing cabinet, gave Amy a significant glance. 'Doesn't exactly look the ecstatic bride-to-be, does she?' she commented in a loud whisper. 'What do you think of her?'

Amy was struggling with her own very unexpected reactions. 'Difficult to tell on two seconds' acquaintance,' she said, with a casual shrug. She could hardly admit, even to herself, that Fiona had inspired in her a feeling so suspiciously like jealousy that it actually shocked her. It had had nothing to do with her looks—it would never have occurred to her to be jealous of any woman who happened to be prettier than she was—but it did have something to do with that air of careless confidence about Fiona, and with the ring on her finger. Those two things seemed suddenly to bring into focus for Amy all that had fallen out of her own life—some measure of security, and someone to care about her, to whom she was unique and special the way she had been to her parents. Or the way she would be to a lover.

'She never used to be so offhand,' Zoe was saying disapprovingly. 'The first couple of times she came here, just before they were engaged, she used to chat a bit, and seem interested in what we were doing. I suppose now she's marrying him she doesn't think she's got to make such an effort.'

Jacquie joined them.

'They're having a row in there!'

'Gosh, you mean real insults?' Zoe enquired eagerly.

'I'm not sure—it's gone suspiciously quiet, but the level of chat sounds as though it's pretty intense. I heard a few bits—she said something about "I don't see why you had to arrange it for that weekend. You know it's so important to me!"' Her attempt to mimic Fiona came out as a comic stage whisper. 'I couldn't hear anything Julius said, though.'

'He's got some sort of a business meeting at the end of next week. She probably wanted him to go to a dance instead,' Zoe offered, and then broke off abruptly.

The door of Julius's office had opened. Zoe started guiltily, but Jacquie showed the presence of mind to tug open the drawer of a filing cabinet. Julius looked grim, and Amy, feeling a little guilty herself, had the misfortune to meet his eyes.

'Two cups of coffee, Amy, please—since you've got time on your hands.'

She had the grace to look abashed, and then there was an audible remark from inside the office.

'I don't want any.'

Julius's expression didn't change. '*One*, Amy, please. Now.'

The door half closed, and then opened again abruptly. This time he caught Zoe with her mouth wide open, on the very first syllable of a comment.

'Time is money, Zoe. Time is measured in office work. No time—no money.' He didn't sound in the least amused.

The door shut again, and Jacquie breathed out a low whistle into the files. Zoe was scarlet, and her eyes began to water.

Amy, in silence, made her way to the kitchen. She was nervous at the idea of interrupting whatever it was going on in Julius's office, but if she delayed giving him the coffee until Fiona had left it might only cause further unpleasantness. With Julius in a mood like that, she was actually scared of him. Scared because if he lost his temper and chose unfairly to take it out on her, with the inexplicable way she was feeling just now she might react unwisely enough to lose her job. She tapped at the door.

Julius was sitting casually at his desk, his long legs stretched out in front of him, and his chair swivelled sideways towards Fiona, who was by the window half perched on the radiator. The expression on his face at least was pleasant when it was directed at Amy herself.

Fiona was frowning.

You could have cut the atmosphere with the proverbial knife, Amy thought as she made her escape after the most perfunctory of introductions. They must be having a monumental row, even if they weren't shouting or throwing things at each other!

'What's going on?' Jacquie hissed at her *en passant*—the files excuse was wearing thin after five minutes.

Amy shrugged, and raised her eyes to heaven. She felt disinclined all of a sudden to discuss any of the private affairs of her boss.

Fiona left not long after that, looking to neither left nor right of her, presumably only too aware of the interest excited by her departure.

In between answering the telephone calls and typing correspondence the rest of the morning, Amy managed to write out a shopping list under cover of a file—and to discover, after a lot of surreptitious rooting around in her bag, that she'd forgotten her sandwiches for lunch.

After a second lunch-hour spent pushing a supermarket trolley up and down the shelves she was marginally more discreet about her three carrier bags when she got back to the office again. One bag under the desk, one behind her chair, and only one left in full view of the phantom clients. At least she wouldn't have to shop tomorrow.

By three o'clock she was starving. The Stock Exchange seemed to have quietened down a bit for the day, Julius had gone out, and the phone calls were easing off. She'd forgotten to buy any sandwiches, but with six Jamaica ginger cakes stuffed into one bag—destined for the Orton village Horticultural Society party that evening—there was a quick and easy answer to her problem.

She took out one Cellophane-wrapped cake and started to undo it. It was, predictably, very sticky, and breaking it with her fingers would scatter crumbs all over her desk. She pushed the remains of the day's correspondence out of the way, smoothed out a paper bag to act as a plate, and then, unwilling to go all the way through the boardroom to fetch proper cutlery from the kitchen, decided to use a ruler as an impromptu knife. It was just as functional in the circumstances, and she could wash it afterwards.

She cut off a small piece of cake and wolfed it down as she stapled a couple of documents together—no one could accuse her of idling. She really was ravenous—at least one of those quiches she'd taken out of the freezer this morning would be reaching the horticulturalists tonight minus a slice. She'd have no time to cook anything when she got home. Pity Charlie had no ambitions to become a chef.

Aware of a change in the light, she looked up, and then froze in the act of sawing off a large lump of ginger cake with the ruler.

Oh, no. Not again.

'Is there something the matter with you, Amy?' Julius enquired politely.

'Er—no... What sort of thing?' she asked foolishly.

'Trouble with your hearing, for example?'

The light sarcasm in his tone made her skin prickle. She was in no doubt as to what he meant.

'I'm sorry—I didn't have time for lunch. I had to do all this shopping.'

'So I see.'

'It won't happen again.' Well, not until next week. She crossed her fingers in her lap, and saw him glance with interest at the supermarket carrier bag. Three other ginger cakes were sticking out of the top. His gaze transferred itself to her, and she met his look defiantly. She couldn't read the look in his eyes this time—but it wasn't quite the same as before.

'Are you *sure* there isn't anything the matter with you?' he asked again. 'You look very pale to me.'

What business was it of his what colour she was? 'I don't wear any make-up,' she replied.

'I noticed. But you don't seem to have a very healthy diet, if what you eat in these offices is anything to judge by.'

'I told you,' she explained patiently. 'I didn't have time to eat a proper lunch because I had to go shopping.' The phone rang then, and for the first time that day she picked it up with a sense of relief. Luckily it was for Julius, and when he disappeared into his office she stuffed the rest of her slice of cake into her mouth and scrunched up the paper bag, dusting any stray crumbs off her desk as she did so. Then she made for the washroom.

Jacquie came in as she was running the tap and holding the sticky ruler underneath the jet of water.

'Are you all right?' Jacquie asked quickly.

Amy looked at her in surprise. 'You're the second person who's just asked me that! What is it—a conspiracy?'

To her amazement, Jacquie actually blushed. 'No of course not!' she said quickly. 'It's just that Julius told me to find you—he thought...you looked a bit odd, that's all.'

'What sort of *odd*?' she demanded.

'Well, you know, pale,' Jacquie said.

Amy shook the water off the ruler, examined it minutely for sticky crumbs and then dried it on the roller towel. 'I should think I am pale!' she announced decisively. 'I have naturally white skin, I don't wear any make-up and there's not much point in a redhead trying to sunbathe—even if I did have the time for it. Which I don't. Unlike his beloved Fiona. Also, I got about five hours' sleep last night because there was a mountain of washing-up to do before going to bed and then the cat woke me up this morning at six o'clock. But anyway, I don't see what any of it has got to do with Julius Prior—apart from the fact that he told me not to eat sandwiches in the reception area yesterday.'

'I hope you're not offended.' Jacquie sounded anxious now. 'He was only . . . well, a bit concerned. He can be very nice, you know. I think he feels sort of protective towards you——'

'Protective!' Amy nearly exploded. '*Him*? He almost gave me a nervous breakdown yesterday, the way he kept pouncing on me for letters and making me answer the phone when I hadn't a clue who were clients and who were brokers or anything!'

'Shh! He'll hear you!'

Amy tossed her red hair and opened her slanting eyes wide at Jacquie in the mirror. 'I don't care if he does!' she declared. 'And if he wants to give me the sack after two days, let him! He owes me for overtime anyway!'

And she marched out. She half expected to find him waiting for her outside, but an examination of the switchboard revealed that he was still on the phone. Then she wasn't sure why she'd got so worked up.

The Horticultural party hadn't offered much in the way of interest, she thought with a yawn as the proceedings dragged to their close in the Orton village hall. She would have much preferred to go home early, but part of the deal she and Jess had struck with the organisers had been that they would stay to do the clearing up at the end. The booking had been arranged through Jess's mother, Celia Bailey, and she had managed to get them double the fee on the condition that they stay. They had planned the menu, although they hadn't had to do all the cooking, and now much of the clearing involved sorting dishes that were named on the bottom so that they could go back to their rightful owners. They had to be stacked in cardboard boxes to be taken away by the organising committee. Nothing could be left in the hall. It was all very boring.

I bet the glamorous Fiona's never had to do anything like this for her living, she thought glumly. You can't stay beautiful and healthy-looking if you're up till midnight with your hands in the sink!

'I'll never get up for work tomorrow,' she told Jess, smothering another enormous yawn. 'Wake me if I fall asleep in the washing-up—I'd like to be unconscious for a week. Thank heaven we don't have another booking for a while! I can't believe I've packed so much action into two days—I only went for the interview on Monday.'

'That's what comes of taking a job with a slave-driver. How was it today, by the way? I haven't had time to ask and I've been dying for the next instalment!'

Between herself and Jess there was the easy familiarity of old schoolfriends, and they were accustomed to sharing most of the events of their lives. Although much of their communication was trivial, it didn't mean that the level of their relationship was in any way superficial.

'*Don't* ask!' she groaned. 'I'll explain to you about that missing ginger cake some time when I've got more energy.'

'Oh.' Jess sounded suddenly doubtful. 'Maybe this isn't quite the time, then to broach the subject...'

'Broach what subject?'

'About that booking on Friday week... I've got the most enormous favour to ask...'

Jess's 'favour' turned out to be a desperate plea to Amy to manage the dinner on her own—her boyfriend Keith had unexpectedly been asked to a friend's dance down in Cornwall, where they would be staying the weekend, and that meant leaving on Friday afternoon.

'I'll do all the shopping and preparation!' she promised. 'All you'll have to do is the basic cooking and maybe serve it—Mum wasn't sure about that when she took the phone message. Please, Ames!'

'OK,' Amy agreed, with another yawn. 'At least I'll get one weekend before it so I can *sleep*.'

Jess hugged her ecstatically. 'Thanks—you're a darling! I promise I'll do the same for you when you meet the love of your life!'

The love of your life... Once again, chance'd be a fine thing! Worry about money and finding work, and making a home for herself and Charlie hadn't left much time even to think about going out with anybody just recently, let alone put it into practice.

She had, of course, been firmly convinced at least once in the past that she'd met the love of her life—only to find she hadn't. The most serious candidate had been Robert, though their student affair hadn't lasted beyond one summer. Afterwards, she'd adopted a philosophical attitude towards its decline. Two nineteen-year-olds couldn't really have known what they'd been about anyway. But Robert had been the type she thought appealed to her—rather laid-back, with a good sense of humour, although too lazy ever really to get anywhere with his future. A total contrast in fact to someone like the dynamic Julius, who never seemed to waste a moment. Not that her boss didn't have a sense of humour too, on occasions, but whereas her mental image of Julius was of a dark-haired figure striding across a street or office, almost crackling with static, her recurrent memory of Robert pictured him lying loose-limbed and lazy on her parents' vast lawn, a book over his face to keep the sun off when he couldn't be bothered to read any longer.

Probably, in the end, he'd have driven her mad. Even their eventual parting had been without drama—Rob had never had a full-scale row with anyone in his life, whereas she enjoyed a few sparks now and then.

Love, she thought ruefully, was definitely a luxury, something which needed time and energy. And both of those were at a premium—especially with a teenage brother to look after.

It was when she and Jess were about to drive home that Celia found them, and Amy was reminded again of Charlie—but in a rather disturbing way.

Celia kissed Amy through the open passenger window and flapped a hand at her daughter. 'Hello, Amy, darling—it's a bit late to stop for a chat now, but I hope that handsome boss of yours isn't working you too hard! Jess told me all about your new job—and I must say James sounds gorgeous——'

'Julius, Mum.'

'Well, Julius, then. I'm hopeless with names.'

Amy grinned. 'My boss is called Dennis. He's forty-five, married, and has two dogs and three children! Jess has been pulling your leg again.'

Celia gave her infectious bubbling laugh. 'I don't be-lieve it—I'm going to come in and see for myself one of these days! By the way, give my love to Charlie and tell him I've got a chocolate cake for the weekend. I saw him in Oxford on Monday morning but he didn't see me——'

'On Monday?' What was Charlie doing in Oxford on Monday? He should have been in school...

'Oh, I expect he was wandering about on some class project. They all do that now—most of the time, it seems to me. Must dash—bye, love. Don't work too hard.'

It was the second time someone had mentioned Charlie's being in Oxford at an unorthodox hour.

Although it was after midnight by the time Amy got home, reluctantly—because if Charlie was playing truant she didn't really want to have to deal with it, and ignorance just at the moment was comparative bliss—she checked her brother's room before she went to bed. He was asleep.

She would have to remember to ask a carefully phrased question about class trips tomorrow, but right now she felt as though she'd been granted a reprieve.

There was no time to ask any sort of questions the next morning, however. It was Charlie himself who woke her, shaking her very urgently by the shoulders and bellowing in her ear.

'*Wake up!*'

Her eyes flew open. 'What time is it? Have I missed the bus?'

Her brother slackened his hold on her and made for the door, hitching up a pair of baggy pyjama trousers and saying something as he went. He never wore a jacket, and his boy's back looked narrow and somehow too bony and white. Seeing him like that, she wished suddenly and passionately that she could take them both on holiday, somewhere hot, where they had nothing to do but swim, and lie in the sun, and eat.

' . . . been ringing for the last ten minutes, and she said you told her to because you'd never get up otherwise.' The last words were no more than a mumble as Charlie disappeared round the bedroom door.

Faithful Jess! What time was it, for heaven's sake?

'Tell her *thanks*!' she yelled.

She had exactly twelve minutes to get to the bus stop. The total silence that met her last instruction was instantly suspicious. 'And Charles Thompson, don't you dare go back to bed!'

She nearly fell asleep on the bus. By lunchtime she didn't know how she was going to keep her eyes open if she didn't get just half an hour's sleep somehow. Taking dictation, even from the easy-paced Dennis, had been an ordeal. Luckily there had been no sign of Julius, and his desk diary, kept by Jacquie, told her that he would be out until the afternoon. If she could only find somewhere to lie down for a few minutes she might make it through till five o'clock!

For the first time she envied the executive status of her two employers. If she'd been one of them she would have had an office to lie down in, and a door to close between herself and the rest of the world—or, alternatively, a luxurious car like Julius's, and she could have gone to sleep across the front seats. But with nothing but the reception area carpet to stretch out upon in full view of office staff, visiting clients, and the decorators who were now working on the stairwell, her only option was a park bench. If she could find one.

When her turn for lunch-break came, she wandered outside with no very clear plan—maybe walking around for a while would wake her up. It was a cold, windy day, but quite bright. If she could sit somewhere sheltered to eat her sandwiches there might even be some warmth in the sun. Then at the end of the street she saw the church.

It had an old porch, with stone benches down each side, and little latticed windows which would keep out the wind. The porch had no outer door and was always open, although the church itself was locked. Surely the vicar wouldn't mind if she went and sat there for half an hour?

There was no one around. A long glancing beam of sunlight fell in one corner of the porch, warming the grey stone seat. With a sigh, she settled herself in the angle of the walls, initially resisting the temptation to put her feet up, and stuffing her carrier bag behind her as a makeshift cushion. She was facing the wide entrance in case the vicar should come along; it would give

her time to gather her wits for polite conversation. She
could see the neatly mown graveyard with its tall, now
leafless trees growing by the wall. She could even see the
Georgian building which housed the offices of Prior
Harding in the wide street just beyond. The white pillars
of the porch also had the sun on them.

She shut her eyes, turning her head a little so that the
light wouldn't fall directly on her closed lids. But the
dusty cobwebbed lattices softened the wintry sun, and
the warmth of the beams fell like a caress on her face.

After a few minutes, she stretched her legs out,
crossing her feet at the ankles, wriggled a little more
comfortably against the carrier bag, and fell asleep.

She was fully aware that she was dreaming—even
telling herself at the time, This is a dream, and feeling
rather resentful that a much needed sleep should be
wasted by a replay of life in the office. Only it wasn't
exactly that; it was a confused jumble of the office, and
Charlie, and burning a dinner she was cooking for a
hundred people. And just when everything had reached
a terrible crisis Julius was there...

He seemed to be telling her to wake up, and although
she was surprised that he didn't sound at all angry she
thought she was telling him—very argumentatively—that
the office floor was as good a place to sleep as any and
that she wasn't going to miss her bus. And then to her
astonishment he kissed her, properly, on the mouth. But
before she had time to think about what it was like he
was saying her name again—'Amy...Amy!' more urgently this time, and reluctantly, very reluctantly, as
though her eyelashes were made of lead and because she
didn't want to have to leave the dream in which Julius
had kissed her just yet, her lids fluttered open.

She was staring into grey eyes that looked down with
concern into her own...lucid, unmistakable grey, their

outer iris ringed with darkness. Eyes fringed with black lashes . . .

Dazedly she pushed her hair back from her forehead, and struggled to sit up. Someone's hand gripped her shoulder.

'Are you all right?'

It was Julius's voice—the real Julius, in the flesh!

He was suddenly there, very alive, his face inches from her own, the pressure of his fingers biting into her through the light jacket she was wearing. She could see the pores of his skin, the way his eyebrows grew unevenly, the way the tips of his lashes were lighter than their roots, and the way the lines of his firm mouth curved with a little kink, exactly marking the centre of that smooth masculine curve of his lower lip. She couldn't take her eyes away from his mouth . . . And then her face flooded with colour as she remembered the dream she'd been woken from—what on earth would he think of her if he could read her mind now?

She stared up at him, her own eyes an intense blue, and, as though suddenly mesmerised by her, he stared back. She wasn't even sure she caught his next words— they were too indistinct—but then, very clearly this time, 'Amy, are you properly awake?'

She pulled herself together.

'Yes—yes, of course I am!' she said abruptly, and her voice seemed unnaturally loud. 'What are you doing here?'

He stood up to his full height.

'I saw you from the road when I was on my way into the office. That scarlet skirt you're wearing is very eye-catching. You're the first redhead I've ever met who could wear a colour like that and get away with it.' His eyes were appraising, as though he was really seeing *her*— not a rather eccentric and inefficient secretary he happened to have employed, but Amy Thompson, red hair, long legs, blue eyes and all. Then he said, 'Are you sure you're all right? Isn't this a slightly peculiar way to pass your lunch-hour—sleeping in a church porch?'

'I just haven't had too much sleep lately, that's all,' she said rather crossly. He was disconcerting her, looking at her like that, and although she wasn't going to admit it she certainly didn't feel wonderful, having been woken suddenly from a deep sleep.

One of those dark eyebrows she had just examined so closely was raised in query. 'Energetic social life?'

'Yes.' Her eyes met his again, defiantly this time. As far as he was concerned, 'social life' was whatever she did out of office hours. It was no business of his if she chose to make money in that time. She swung her legs off the stone bench with an energy she had to dredge up from a very deep inner well indeed.

'You can't burn the candle at both ends for too long, you know, Amy.'

She searched his face for the criticism she felt sure must be lurking there—the words had sounded too disarmingly gentle.

'I don't,' she said shortly. His expression was enigmatic. 'And this is my lunch-hour.'

A wry grin twisted that rather fascinating mouth. 'As I think I've pointed out to you before, and at the risk of sounding boring, *lunch*-hours have a very obvious purpose.' He glanced down at the supermarket bag. 'Shopping again?'

She reached for it hastily, only to find her wrist unexpectedly circled by strong, lean fingers.

'I'll carry it for you,' Julius said. It was less an offer than a statement.

She stood up unsteadily. He took the bag in the same hand as his briefcase, and she felt his other hand under her elbow as he guided her to the porch entrance and down the path to the church gate. It must be because of her dream that she was so uncomfortably aware of his closeness to her every step of the way.

'Do you spend every lunch-hour shopping for food?' he queried lightly. He probably thought she would be on her way to the supermarket again. The bag was far too big for its contents—a small packet of sandwiches and a thick extra jersey she had brought to the office.

'Not all of them. But I'm buying for the freezer.' The glib lie occurred to her on the spur of the moment.

'Hungry freezer.'

The comment was uttered in a perfectly neutral tone, but her reply was on the defensive again. 'I've got to do a lot of entertaining soon, and I'd rather get all the shopping over with.'

'I suppose Charlie eats quite a lot?'

Charlie? How should he know about——? Oh, yes, of course. She'd let him think Charlie was someone she was living with on a rather different basis from the true one.

She gave an involuntary little shiver as a gust of wind blew across them, and it seemed to wake her up. They were walking slowly towards the church gate now. Sideways, her slanting glance caught his eye. She didn't quite know why she wanted to keep up this fiction about Charlie, but she did.

'Yes,' she said. 'He does. I think he'd be happy if I spent my entire life chained to the stove cooking mounds of chips and beefburgers.' That, at least, was true.

She couldn't read Julius's expression, but his tone was perfectly clear—disapproving. 'Not a very imaginative eater, your Charlie, is he?'

Why should he disapprove? It didn't make any difference to him! 'No,' she agreed. 'He isn't.'

'And what about you, Amy, what do you like to eat?'

'Anything,' she admitted.

The look in his eye as they waited at the kerb for a gap in the traffic was openly sceptical. 'Well, now is the time to prove it,' he said slowly, 'I'm taking you to lunch.'

Lunch! But——! She glanced at her watch. She must have slept for nearly half an hour. She had about twenty minutes before she had to get back to the office. And what about Julius?

'I thought you were having lunch with Fiona today!' she protested, rather ungraciously.

'We had to cancel it. Now I'm having lunch with you. Which do you prefer—the King's Arms or the Crown?'

'I—er—I don't mind. I've never been in either.' In the two days she'd spent working in Wychford, she'd hardly had time to notice that there were any pubs, let alone go in them.

She was beginning to believe it must all be a continuation of her dream as he steered her towards the Crown, sat her down at a table in the dining area, and put a menu in front of her.

'But I have to get back to the office!' she protested again. 'I can't be late!'

'Yes, you can, you're with me.'

'But Dennis——'

He ignored her objections, glancing at the menu. 'Have you any preferences, or shall I order?'

She would have to have something she could eat quickly. 'Sandwiches?'

'They don't serve sandwiches at lunchtime.'

That was odd, because they were on the menu. Still, if he'd been here before he must know.

'Salad, then?'

'The salads are finished by this time.'

'How do you know? You haven't even asked!'

'Do you like steak and kidney pie?'

'Yes, but——'

She didn't have a chance to say any more, because he was halfway to the bar.

They were served immediately with huge plates of steaming pie and gravy, with an assortment of vegetables, and Julius brought back a large glass of orange juice for her from the bar.

'You said you ate anything!' he challenged her, a half-smile on his face.

'I do,' she assured him. 'But why are we doing this?' Maybe she was still dreaming!

'Because it's lunchtime, and I'm hungry even if you're not. And I'm beginning to think you need some looking after. Eat as much as you want—leave the rest if it's too much.'

'I thought you said nobody did any "nannying" at Prior's?' she queried, unable to resist the temptation to point out his inconsistency.

He smiled at her again. 'Boss's privilege.'

But the steak and kidney pie wasn't too much, and she had a pudding after that—apple pie with cream. She should have been ashamed of herself, but she'd discovered once the food was on the table that she was really too hungry to care.

She caught Julius watching her from time to time, and wondered why he should find the sight of her eating her lunch so fascinating. If it hadn't all been so unreal, she would have felt very awkward in his company. Because of the dream, she was suddenly aware of him in a way she hadn't been before. He really was a very attractive man. She was beginning to understand now exactly what Zoe saw in him.

He ordered coffee.

They hadn't spoken much during the meal, only a few passing comments about the morning's business, and the office in general. He'd asked her if she liked working for Prior's and she'd been as diplomatic as she could in her replies. She got the feeling that he knew she was being evasive.

Then the conversation took an unexpected turn. He said, 'It must have been a great shock to you when your parents were killed—a flying accident, I think you told me?'

Was this why he had asked her to have lunch with him? To find out more about those suspicious gaps in her c.v. so that he could make up his mind whether to keep her on or not after the two months were up? But it wasn't just that she still found it hard to talk about her parents in any but the most general terms—talking about the accident to Julius could mean she revealed too much about the home problems he'd been so determined she shouldn't have.

'They were on holiday in Kenya,' she said reluctantly. 'They were staying with friends. One day they chartered a small plane to fly over a game reserve. They had engine trouble. The pilot was killed too.'

'And the friends?'

'They weren't with them.'

She stared into her coffee-cup, avoiding looking at him, but she knew he was looking at her. There was a brief silence, then he said, 'What happened to your father's business, Amy?'

After the lunch he'd just bought her, she felt obliged to reply. Maybe he'd been counting on that.

'It went into liquidation.'

'Why?'

She sighed impatiently. 'It's all rather complicated. I don't really understand it well enough to explain.'

That wasn't quite true. It was the subject of her father she felt she couldn't do justice to.

'Try.'

She began to fiddle with an empty sugar packet, aware that once Julius was in inquisition mode he couldn't be fobbed off with easy answers.

'Matlock and West were in property—they owned the leases on a lot of business premises, and it was Dad who ran the company. Some time before the accident, he'd decided they needed to expand—widen their interests a bit—and he'd tied up a lot of money including his own in a holiday development scheme...'

'And?'

'There were a lot of problems—objections to parts of the development when they'd already started building, delays with contractors, a rise in interest rates which meant difficulty with financing the bank loans... When Dad died things had got to a critical stage. The bank wanted more collateral and he'd already put up our house against the loan. He'd gone out to Kenya in the first place to see if he could persuade this friend to go into some other business venture, which might have helped to finance the development scheme in the long run. I don't know what would have happened if he'd lived— maybe he could have pulled it off. He said all he needed was time...'

'What happened to you after the accident?'

'Everything was sold—the house, the furniture, everything. We'd had a big house, with quite a lot of land, but it couldn't possibly meet the debts. The bank decided after that to write off Dad's personal liabilities, and the company was wound up.'

'But what about insurance policies?'

Yes, that was the key to the whole thing. How could you explain to someone without sounding critical of the father you'd adored that there were no insurance policies? Anyway, not the sort that would make provision for a family in the event of his death.

Nick Thompson had been one of the most charming men who had ever walked the earth—full of life, humour, and endless schemes; a born risk-taker. As such, he'd have done better to remain single rather than marry at twenty-three a girl four years younger than himself. Amy had been born within the first year of the marriage, and her family's lifestyle had swung from one extreme to another ever since. Sometimes they had had no money, sometimes they had had lots.

Convinced he'd end up a millionaire, her father had lost one fortune on the Stock Exchange by the age of twenty-six, and then set out to make another. He'd taken hair-raising risks, and cut every corner he could while staying just inside the law. Sometimes it had paid off, sometimes it hadn't. When she was old enough to realise what sort of a man he was, she'd used to wonder how her mother could remain so calm and happy in the face of the continual crises. It had been like living on a roller-coaster.

But for Joanne Thompson the sun had shone out of Nick, and if she'd seen his faults, as far as she was concerned they were more than outweighed by his virtues. The only thing she'd insisted on was that Amy and her brother should be educated at good schools—what they chose to do with their lives after that was up to them.

But how could she explain any of this to a man like Julius? It was better not to try. The cold facts could never do justice to her father, and like her mother she wouldn't have wanted him any other way, for all his faults. She still couldn't talk about her parents without that pain coming into the back of her throat, and the pricking of tears in her eyes.

Julius was studying her, waiting for her answer. She avoided his look.

'There weren't any insurance policies,' she said abruptly. 'Which is why I need to work for you.'

She glanced pointedly at her watch, and gave him a very mechanical version of her witchy smile, again without meeting his eyes. 'Thank you for a wonderful lunch. Do you think I could go back to the office now?'

If he was taken aback by her reply, he didn't show it. He continued to consider her. Then he said, 'I don't think we've finished this conversation, Amy, but you're right— I'd better not keep you any later...' He appeared to hesitate for a moment about something. Then to her astonishment he put his hand over hers where it was lying on the table. 'Amy, I know I said I wanted to employ people who could give their time to the job, but if you have any problems you will tell me, won't you?'

Amy stared at the lean fingers lying over her own. The light, warm touch seemed to be doing strange things to her. It meant comfort, and reassurance, and strength— all the things she was most in need of, and couldn't afford to seek from this man who so unexpectedly appeared to be offering them to her.

'Oh, yes,' she assured him insincerely. 'It's very kind of you, but really there aren't any problems— none at all!'

CHAPTER FOUR

ONCE Julius had disappeared into his office, Jacquie immediately found an excuse to join her in the cloakroom where she was dragging a comb through her hair. She must have looked a mess in the pub—her hair seemed to have knotted itself into an unruly red tangle. She tried to switch her mind on to the afternoon's work, but it wasn't easy to dismiss what had just happened—especially with the inquisitive Jacquie at her elbow.

'Where were you? Zoe's still at lunch. We thought something must have happened. Did you meet Julius while you were out?'

'Sort of. He took me to the Crown—I couldn't get away before.'

'Oh, it didn't matter—things were pretty slack. But I thought Julius was supposed to be seeing Fiona!'

Amy explained briefly, leaving out the bit about the church porch.

'What did you eat?' Jacquie asked curiously.

Amy was both amused and irritated. 'What is this interest everybody has in my diet? Honestly, you're as bad as Julius. He never took his eyes off me—and he never even let me order. I suppose after catching me cutting up that bit of ginger cake with a ruler yesterday he wanted to see if I knew what to do with a knife and fork.'

Jacquie looked at her awkwardly, as though she couldn't quite make up her mind about something. 'No—not really. It's nothing like that...' She hesitated, and then plunged on, 'He was just afraid you might be ill.

You know—that you might be bulimic or whatever it's called.'

'*Bulimic*!' They would probably be able to hear her all over the offices, but she didn't care. The amusement had gone all of a sudden—this gave a whole new meaning to the impromptu lunch date! 'What *on earth* gave him that idea?'

'Shh! He'll hear you!' warned Jacquie desperately. 'I wasn't supposed to tell you! But you must admit you are very thin and you do seem to buy an awful lot of food at the supermarkets and then you eat three sandwiches for lunch all at once—well, that's what Julius said anyway...'

It wasn't just the thought of an office conspiracy going on behind her back that upset her, it was Julius himself—trust him to have an ulterior motive! And she'd thought it might be just because he wanted her company. Well, no, she hadn't. Secretly it was what she would have liked to think, but he'd made it clear he was interested in finding out about her background. So it wasn't only the c.v. that concerned him—he wanted to make sure she wouldn't faint in the middle of taking a vital letter. Very inconvenient. 'Time is money, Zoe!' It might cut his profit margins.

'I suppose you're in here now to make sure I don't make myself sick or something!' she accused.

From Jacquie's guilty expression she knew she'd got it right. She gave her hair such a furious tug with the comb that it made her eyes smart.

'I have a very busy life outside this office—not problematic,' she added quickly, 'just *busy*. I have someone to feed at home, lots of social things going on——' that was deliberately misleading but true '—and I don't have enough time to sit about eating nice little lunches. And some people are naturally skinny!' It wasn't really fair to take it out on Jacquie—it was Julius she should be going for.

Jacquie looked quite upset. 'But Amy, he was very concerned about you!'

'Well, he doesn't have to concern himself with me!' said Amy emphatically. 'And you can assure him of that!'

By the time she'd caught the bus home she'd simmered down a bit, and spent most of the journey through the cold November darkness analysing just why she'd made such a fuss about it. Jess, knowing the way she could never resist picking at things when she was cooking, would think the idea of her starving herself very funny. Perhaps it was, in the circumstances. Except that it really hurt to be made to see, quite so effectively, that to Julius she was just an employee. It wasn't Amy the person he was concerned about, but Miss Thompson the secretary who might be ill and let them all down in a crisis. She thought of the dream she'd had in the church porch, and that, for some reason, made her more miserable.

It's because I'm tired, she told herself dismally. Thank heaven there aren't any more dinner bookings until the end of next week, even if it doesn't mean so much money.

Saturday was a blissful oasis after the struggles of the week, and she and Charlie went over to Jess's for Sunday lunch, which meant that she didn't have to cook. Nobody thought to mention Charlie's unexpected trip to Oxford on a school day, and when it occurred to her later she put off asking him about it. So what if he had skipped one morning at school? If it were serious, she'd have heard about it by now.

The following week seemed slightly easier—she didn't have to keep asking where everything was. She spent most of her time with Dennis, and Julius seemed to be out a lot. She tried to avoid him when he was there, and was glad she always had a legitimate excuse to be busy typing. He did find her once, though, with her hair caught in the printer. She and Zoe were trying to unwind it from the end of the roller without clogging up the works completely. It only served to deepen her conviction that he must consider her the most inept secretary he'd ever employed.

He stood by the desk, arms folded, watching them both. Amy, painfully aware of him, took no obvious notice, but Zoe went into an apologetic dither.

'It's all right, Zoe—I'll give Amy another two minutes to get out of that, and then I'm coming in here with the scissors.'

Zoe took the hint and went back to her desk, but before Julius left Amy to it he leaned over and said almost in her ear, which caused a little shiver to go down her back, 'Red seaweed, Amy. You know what seaweed's good for? Forecasting rain! I'm looking forward to hanging a bit outside the office window...'

She found that her hands were shaking so much she had even more of a problem extricating herself. Of course he wouldn't have cut her hair off, but it wasn't that that concerned her.

Friday's dinner booking was now going to be a pleasant contrast to the rest of the week, and she found she was actually looking forward to it. It didn't worry her that she'd be coping without Jess—she'd done it before.

The address, not far from Wychford, shouldn't be too difficult to find—assuming Celia had got it right in the first place. She'd confessed she hadn't had a notebook to hand when the call had come through, and had wandered round repeating the details to herself until she'd found one later.

'Don't worry,' she'd assured her daughter. 'I have a mnemonic system that never fails—the only thing I can't remember is the telephone number, which means we can't ring them to check. Never mind, they'll surely contact us again in an emergency.'

Bearing in mind that she just could be going to the wrong address, Amy started packing up Jess's mini-van in good time. There were covered dishes of prepared vegetables, and a casserole of venison that would only need a thorough warming, as well as the ingredients for two other courses. Jess had cooked the pancakes for the crêpes Suzette, and stacked them between layers of greaseproof paper—the least she could do, she said, as her contribution to the evening.

Number 27 Market Street was in an attractive row of old Cotswold stone houses, with large square-paned windows. There were two bells outside it, the upper one labelled 'Newton', so she pushed the lower hopefully. Half an hour's ringing of doorbells looking for someone called 'Abbott' wasn't an appealing prospect.

She glanced at her watch. There were lights on in the lower part of the house. She wondered if she should leave it another minute before she pushed the bell again. It was chilly on the doorstep.

She had her hand raised to ring when she heard a woman's voice saying angrily, 'I don't give a damn what you think!' and seconds later the door was opened. Her hand dropped involuntarily, and her mouth opened in dismay. Jess's mother *had* got the wrong address. Fiona Harper-Maxwell was standing on the doorstep.

'Oh,' Amy said, startled. 'I'm so sorry! I was looking for someone called Mr Abbott.'

The expression on Fiona's face was one of neutrality achieved with effort—she must have been having the row with someone inside—and the light in her eyes was mutinous until it changed into something like recognition.

'You're one of Julius's secretaries, aren't you?'

'Er—yes. But I seem to have come to the wrong house. I'm so sorry to have bothered you.' Was this where Fiona lived? Didn't she have a flat in London? Or——

Then a familiar male voice said, 'Who is it?'

Julius!

Panic seized her. She could hardly ask him about the Mr Abbott she was supposed to be cooking for, with the Cookery Unlimited van parked so ostentatiously on the other side of the road! She'd have to pretend it had nothing to do with her——

'It's all right!' she said quickly to Fiona. 'I've remembered where I ought to be. I'm sorry——'

And she was just on the point of flight when Julius said, 'Amy! What on earth are you doing here?'

For a split-second she was tempted to run away despite the fact that he'd seen her. Then, very reluctantly, she turned back to find him standing just behind Fiona, hands on hips, looking more casual than she'd ever seen him. One of his familiar striped office shirts was loosely tucked into a pair of jeans that hugged his lean hips closely, and the sleeves of his shirt were rolled up to the elbows. He was barefooted.

Amy's heart gave an uncomfortable jolt, and she stared at him as though she'd never seen him before. She tried to gather her wits.

'I've—er—come to the wrong house!' she said desperately. 'Sorry to have bothered you both.'

Julius looked as surprised to see her as she was to see him—but he didn't look horrified. She wondered if any of her true feelings about the situation showed in her face, and hoped they didn't.

'Who were you looking for—a friend?' He sounded very curious.

'Not—not exactly. Somebody called Mr Abbott.'

He thrust out his lower lip doubtfully. 'No one of that name in this street that I know of. What does he do?'

'I've no idea.' She glanced at Fiona; her expression of polite interest only just masked whatever it was underneath. 'It's all right. I forgot where he lives. But I remember now.' That sounded very silly.

'Where *does* he live?'

Trust Julius to want the awkward details! Amy waved her hand vaguely towards one end of the street. 'Down there.'

She saw his eyes flicker quickly in the direction she had indicated, and then a rather amused expression came over his face.

Just then Fiona said politely, but with a certain finality, 'I hope you find him.' She gave a fleeting but unconvincing smile in Amy's direction, presumably a token leave-taking, turned and pushed past Julius into the hall, disappearing through a door.

Julius folded his arms, the way he did in the office, and leant against the side of the door. He was looking at her in a way that made her nervous; he seemed to find something in the situation very humorous.

'Funny you should turn up tonight, Amy.'

'Oh?' But she didn't intend to wait for the answer. 'I'm sorry, I'm in an awful hurry. I——'

'That van parked on the other side of the road—it wouldn't have anything to do with you, would it?'

She didn't need to look at it—he must have guessed. But she wasn't going to give it away if she didn't have to—even if it meant hiding round the corner of Market Street to creep back unseen later on, and drive herself to the nearest phone box to contact Celia.

'Why do you ask?' she said, as innocently as she could manage.

He was grinning at her now, clearly enjoying some private joke, and just before he spoke she got a terrible feeling she knew what it was.

'Your Abbott wouldn't be a *Prior* by any chance, would he?'

Oh, no. Darling muddle-headed Celia! she thought despairingly. Of all the unlucky mnemonics...! But there wasn't much she could do about it now.

'Actually——' She took a deep breath. 'Actually, if you're waiting for someone to cook dinner for you, it's me.'

She met his eyes squarely this time. Julius, still leaning casually against the doorpost, stared at her now with a mixture of amusement and fascination. Then he said, 'Where's the other half? I thought there were two of you.'

'She couldn't make it.'

She had a strong suspicion that he believed her responsible for confusing the details of the booking, and she couldn't bear him to think her more of an idiot than she must appear at the office.

Even though it seemed a rather treacherous betrayal of Celia's ineptitude, she found herself saying, 'My friend's mother takes the bookings for us as a favour. She didn't have anything to write on.'

He continued to look at her. There was something in his eyes now that she hadn't seen before, and it made her more nervous of him than when he was doing his full tycoon act at work.

They weighed each other up in silence for a while longer. Her heart-rate seemed to have increased by half as much again. What was he going to say about her job at Prior's?

But he only smiled at her, and said, 'I hope your partner's mother remembered to tell you to bring the food. That *was* the arrangement, wasn't it?'

She couldn't resist it. 'Carrier bags full!'

If it had been anybody else, she would have said he was rather embarrassed, despite the grin he gave her.

'I had no idea you went in for this sort of thing. Am I forgiven?'

'You mean for thinking I had some major diet problems, and setting Jacquie and Zoe to spy on me? I was very cross about that!'

'I know. I heard you. Was that why you've been avoiding me for the past week?'

'Oh!' She didn't think he'd noticed, and she didn't want to admit it. So she said rather awkwardly, 'I hope I didn't swear.'

He laughed. 'Not that I remember. You'd better come in, Miss *Witchery* Unlimited.'

He stood back to let her pass him, and she stepped into a wide carpeted hall with doors opening off both sides. An attractive staircase with a carved wooden banister led up to the first floor.

He was standing right behind her, and she was conscious of just how close he was. He showed her where the kitchen was, then he slipped on a pair of shoes, taking the van keys from her while she investigated the cooking facilities, and brought in the boxes. Fiona didn't reappear.

She tried to gather her wits. Just think of this as an ordinary booking, she told herself with desperation. Even if it isn't. And what did he mean by *witchery* exactly?

'OK now?' He slid the last box on to one of the waxed pine work surfaces.

The kitchen, she'd thought with a twinge of envy, was as well equipped and attractively laid out as any she'd ever seen.

'Thanks. Everything's fine. Do you want me to set the table?'

His expression gave nothing away. 'Fiona will do that. Shout if you need anything.'

And he was gone.

His casual tone of dismissal hurt just a bit—it reminded her very effectively yet again that she was Julius's employee and of no interest to him beyond the immediate job he paid her to do. It was Fiona he was concerned about.

But if anyone was going to do any shouting it sounded as though it might be his fiancée. Her opening remark to him was embarrassingly audible. 'I didn't know you employed your secretaries for their cooking talents.' The tone was acidic.

She heard Julius reply, 'Neither did I. Amy's a surprise to us all. Constantly.' And then the door shut.

But she couldn't help being aware of the row that seemed to be developing between them, inadequately muffled by the intervening walls. She could hear the deep tones of Julius's voice from time to time, and although what she said wasn't quite clear Fiona's voice was raised more than once.

Then, 'I can't see why it's so bloody important to you—you could have got out of it if you'd tried! He's supposed to be a friend, isn't he?'

Torn between curiosity and discretion, her finer feelings won and Amy with some reluctance closed the kitchen door and switched on the little portable radio she found on a kitchen shelf. In her place, Jacquie would probably have been encamped in the hall by now. But there was one thing she had made up her mind about: she wasn't going to feed the fires of office gossip with anything that happened tonight. Julius at work was fair game—particularly if he was unwise enough to give his fiancée free run of the building and conduct any of his private concerns on the premises—but his life outside office hours was his own affair. And, to give him his due, he'd registered none of the dismay she might have predicted—or disapproval either—when he'd found her on his doorstep.

She concentrated on preparations for the meal, taking her time. As she wasn't expected to do any extras like setting a dinner-table, she could take it at a more leisurely pace than she'd expected.

Then she heard a door opening.

'Well, I'm going with William—and you can go to *hell*!'

Fiona sounded furious, and she heard Julius say her name quickly. And then the front door slammed.

Oh, dear. Amy was rather ashamed that the thought that came immediately to mind was would that mean an end of the dinner party—and if it did would he still pay her?

Operations suspended, she perched on a kitchen stool, wondering when Julius would reappear. There were no sounds of anyone moving about the house, although through a closed door and with the radio on it wasn't easy to be certain.

Idly, she picked up a tomato. It might be a good idea to start on fiddly decorations like tomato flowers now, in case he did want to go on with the dinner. Where had Fiona gone?

The kitchen door opened, and Julius stood there. He propped himself against the side of the door, one hand in the pocket of his jeans, and looked at her. Carefully she put down the tomato and returned the look.

His expression wasn't exactly grim, but it wasn't too light-hearted either. She didn't know whether she was expected to make any comment or not.

'I suppose you heard that?'

She nodded, flicking one long red strand of hair over her shoulder.

'All of it?' he pursued.

'I heard Fiona leave. And slam the door.' And then she asked carefully, 'Does that mean she won't be setting the table now?'

The rather forbidding expression vanished, and he gave a reluctant smile. 'You've just about summed it up... Have a drink while we review the situation?'

She refused the alcohol he offered, accepting instead a glass of Indian tonic stacked with ice and lemon. She wondered if the double whisky he poured for himself indicated anything about his mood.

He came to stand beside her, watching for a while in silence as she deftly cut long curls of tomato with a sharp knife. She longed to ask about Fiona. She was so aware of him she found it hard to concentrate on what she was doing, and was nervous of cutting her fingers on the knife.

'How is it that when I ring up for a cook I get my secretary in my kitchen?' he asked at last.

She turned to look at him. There was something in that direct, lucid gaze that prompted her for the first time to abandon all thoughts of inventing a quick story to gloss over the truth.

'This is my real job,' she said quietly. 'Jess and I have been working as Cookery Unlimited for nearly a year now. How did you get to hear about us?'

'I saw your advert in the local paper.' He leaned back against the work surface, whisky glass in hand. 'How do you come to be doing this in the first place?'

She flicked back another strand of hair, aware of his eyes on her. 'I did a catering course at college—after a cordon bleu cookery course in London. It's what I wanted.'

'None of this appears on your c.v.'

Her wretched c.v. again... Of course. She couldn't keep the sarcasm out of her reply. 'Would you really have thought the ability to cook sole *Véronique* a recommendation in a secretary?'

'I might have done, if I'd known. We could have started up a new line in directors' lunches.'

It was obvious that was meant to defuse what was becoming a rather tense discussion, and there was a pause while she flayed another tomato, wondering if she dared ask him now if he was going to sack her. She still couldn't assess his reaction to the discovery of her double life.

'Why didn't you tell me?' he asked.

She put down the knife with care and then turned to him, meeting his eyes honestly. 'I was afraid you wouldn't take me on if you thought I had another job. You were very insistent about people with other commitments.'

'And afterwards?'

She shrugged, and looked away. 'The same reason really. I'm still afraid you'll fire me.'

Another silence. Then he asked, 'Where's this Jess of yours?'

She explained about Cornwall, and Jess's boyfriend, and the news that she'd gone to a dance prompted him to explain that Fiona too had left for an old schoolfriend's party in London. There was no suggestion of criticism that she had walked out on the dinner party so suddenly, even though Amy had got the impression that the dinner engagement was vital business as much as pleasure. His apparent understanding of Fiona's feelings was something she admired in him.

'So this is quite an important dinner party tonight?' she asked in cautious tones. She didn't want to make it sound as though she was trying to condemn his fiancée's defection, since he had been so careful to avoid doing so himself. But it would help to be able to assess the evening ahead.

'Chris is an old friend of mine, and he's bringing his wife, Maxine. I thought it would be nice for Fiona to meet them both, and she could get to know Maxine while I plied Chris with drinks in an attempt to get him to put some money into a business enterprise. I was thinking of expanding the Spanish property venture my company started up a couple of years ago.'

'I know.' Her reply was automatic.

He looked at her sharply, almost as though he'd forgotten that he saw her in the office every day.

Then he said slowly, 'Of course you do.'

He was silent for a moment, as though considering the implications of what she'd just said. She took another sip of her tonic, and started to twist the long curls of tomato into rosettes.

'Amy...' It was an uncharacteristically thoughtful beginning. 'I'm going to ask you an enormous favour.'

She raised her eyebrows and waited, but he seemed to be summing her up again.

'OK,' she said at last, with a nervous laugh. 'I'm all agog! What on earth is it? You want me to stretch the meal to another six guests by passing off a local Chinese take-away as my own cooking—or do I do conjuring tricks while I serve the coffee?'

He gave a fleeting grin. 'Nothing so entertaining. No. I want you to join us.'

'You mean to serve the food?'

'I mean to eat it with us. As a friend.'

He must have known that she wasn't in a position to refuse anything reasonable that he could ask. But she found she had mixed feelings at the prospect. Just for the evening, they'd be creating the fiction that she was his friend, and therefore on that level his equal, whereas all the time she was just his employee and tomorrow in the office he'd have no more interest in her than in Jacquie or Zoe—and the thought of that hurt.

Although it wasn't a Cinderella complex that upset her, she looked doubtfully down at her butcher's apron and jeans. 'I'm not dressed for it.'

There was another silence, and she glanced up to find his eyes taking in every contour of her loose sweater and close-fitting jeans that emphasised her long legs despite the unglamorous butcher's apron—she even wondered if he was mentally stripping her. There was something distinctly provocative about the gleam in his eye when he finally met her accusing stare. She was determined she wouldn't let him embarrass her.

'I think you look very sexy underneath that apron,' he said at last. 'But it's up to you. I don't mind what you wear, and I'm certainly not going to dress up.'

That amused her, and he saw her looking at his bare feet—he'd taken his shoes off again.

'Well, not much!'

She bit her lip doubtfully. 'I haven't time to drive home, but I've got something a bit more suitable in the car just in case I was expected to appear in the dining-room.'

'As long as it's not a Victorian maid's outfit, wear what you like.'

She couldn't read whatever it was in his eyes just then, and she turned back to fiddle with the decorations, unaccountably relieved when he finally left the kitchen.

Once she had done as much as she could to prepare for the final cooking stages, she went out to the van to fetch the skirt and top she'd flung in at the last moment.

She decided to change before she had to devote herself entirely to the kitchen.

'Use my bedroom,' Julius offered. 'There's a long mirror in there, and the bathroom's *en suite*.'

She felt very aware that she was entering a personal area of his life as she tried the door to the left of the hall. It opened into what had once been a large reception-room but now contained a double bed.

Conscious of the fact that Julius could walk in when she was only half dressed, Amy decided to use the bathroom to change in, and quickly slipped off her jeans and sweater. The skirt she had brought was black, fairly tight-fitting, and not overlong. The black stretchy top that matched it had three-quarter sleeves and a low neckline that was just respectable. She fished her comb out of her bag and went to survey herself in the long mirror on the back of the wardrobe doors. She was glad she had had time to wash her hair the night before—the long dark red strands reflected a red-gold in the bedroom lights. But she thought her outfit needed something else to turn it from what was reasonably fashionable but functional into evening wear, and when she stretched her arms up to comb her hair there was a compromising glimpse of bare midriff.

A russet-coloured soft suede belt hanging on the hook of the bathroom door had caught her eye—it was not a man's belt. Fiona must have forgotten it in her hurry to leave. She hesitated, disliking the idea of borrowing another woman's things when she wasn't there to ask, but another glance at the precarious waistline persuaded her. She slipped it round her narrow waist, fastening it at the back on the innermost buckle hole. The stiffened front widened into a long, flattering diamond shape. It was ideal for what she wanted, but she supposed she ought to ask Julius if she could wear it.

'Julius?' She emerged from the bedroom to find him in the hall. 'Is it all right if——?'

She faltered into silence, taken aback by the look on his face. He was staring at her with an expression she'd never seen before. Did he disapprove?

'I'm sorry—I'll take it off if you think I shouldn't wear it.'

'Wear what?'

'Fiona's belt.'

'Oh.' He looked as though what she was asking him suddenly made no sense to him. Then he said, 'No. That's fine.'

There was a silence.

She asked anxiously, 'Do I look all right?'

'More than all right,' he said quietly, his eyes directly holding hers. She thought he was going to say something else, but he just looked at her. Then he smiled. 'Can you cook dressed like that?'

She grinned back, relieved that the curious moment had passed. 'Oh, I'll wear the apron. You are sure it's OK about Fiona's belt?'

'I don't think she'd remember it even if she saw it,' he said dismissively. 'That girl has more clothes than anyone I've ever met.'

While she went back into the kitchen, Julius decided to set the table in the other room. She was asked to inspect it when he had finished and followed him into the enormous sitting-room, one end of which served as a dining area. She cast an approving eye over the gleaming silver, and polished mahogany surface of the table.

'What about candles?' she asked. 'Do you have any?'

He bent down to look in the sideboard, and she found herself watching him, the way his shirt was stretched taut across the shoulders as he bent forward, and the way his hair touched the back of his collar, which was open at the neck. He had changed into a pair of dark trousers and clean white shirt and she saw almost with disappointment that he was now respectably shod. There had been something extraordinarily attractive about him wandering around barefoot when she had first arrived. The casual Julius—perhaps even the real Julius—not the office tycoon. She had a sudden overwhelming urge to touch him, and to have him touch her... She gave a little shiver and turned away, shocked by the ridiculous intensity of it.

'It doesn't look like it,' he was saying. 'The last time we had some, Fiona put them away.'

And that remark was like a bucket of cold water thrown over her. It spoke of the casual intimacy of their lives together, and the reminder of the woman who was his fiancée actually hurt. She was an outsider again. His cook for the evening. The 'friendship' was an illusion and would have vanished by tomorrow morning. There would be the office gossip going on around her; he would be on one side of the fence as the boss—and, as one of his secretaries, she would be on the other.

'We've got some in the van. I'll go and get them.' That 'we' was her and Jess, their professional status opposed to the partnership of Julius and Fiona. It was her private defence against the very inconvenient feelings her continued association with Julius seemed to be creating in her.

He must have heard something of it in her tone, and turned his head sharply in surprise.

'What's the matter?'

She watched him straighten up. His perception surprised her. 'Nothing,' she said, her eyes deliberately blank.

'If you give me the keys again, I'll get them. You're not ideally dressed for a cold night in November, are you?'

'Neither are you.'

He gave her a wry smile that eased just a little the unexpected tension building between them.

'Don't argue with me, woman. I've had enough of that for one night.'

Despite her complex reactions to Julius himself, she was far too full of curiosity about his friends to be daunted by the prospect of dinner with them.

Chris was tall and bearded, with the haphazardly ugly looks that were attractive in themselves; next to the slighter, more athletic Julius he looked like a large, friendly troll. Maxine was small and vivacious, her blonde hair cut in a boyish bob. Amy liked both of them immediately.

The introductions were informal and friendly. Julius said nothing about Amy working for him—in any capacity. As far as the others were concerned she was just a friend doing him a favour for the evening because Fiona couldn't be there.

She and Julius worked well together as a team. Without making it obvious, he was there to help when she needed it, quite willing to take instructions from her as though their normal roles had been reversed. She also found that she could slip in and out of the conversation at the table with ease, and all three of them treated her as the friend Julius had claimed her to be.

Later Maxine followed her into the kitchen to help her make coffee.

'That was a super dinner,' she complimented her enthusiastically. 'I bet Julius is always asking you to cook for him when Fiona's not around. I gather she's the proverbial can't-even-boil-an-egg girl.'

Amy smiled, but the topic of Fiona wasn't a welcome one, and she was glad that Julius's absent fiancée had scarcely been mentioned all evening.

She learned from Maxine that the two men had been friends since university days, subsequently travelling the world together collecting a year's worth of hair-raising escapades. When Maxine in turn showed some curiosity about the discussion going on in the living-room between her husband and his friend—the Spanish deal hadn't featured in the conversation over dinner—Amy pretended ignorance of it. Her office knowledge was privileged information.

'Well, all I can say is I hope Chris agrees to whatever it is. Julius has a real Midas touch. The idea of getting very rich quick definitely appeals!'

Amy gave a cautious smile. 'You make it sound as though it's all a bit shady.'

'Good heavens, no! Julius is absolutely straight. He's one of the most honest men I've ever met, and for someone with his range of business interests that's saying a lot.' Then she added, 'He's also one of the kindest.'

Amy saved up that remark to think about later. It undermined quite a lot of the assumptions she'd made about him during their past encounters.

Then Maxine gave her further food for thought.

'We were really quite worried about Julius,' she confided. 'Chris thought he was beginning to organise every aspect of his life like his business. He even suspected he might have run Fiona through a computer program— you know, a sort of checklist of requirements for the ideal young company director's wife! Do you know her well?'

But Amy didn't rise to that one. She was very relieved that she could honestly say that Fiona was the merest acquaintance.

It was late when Chris and Maxine finally left—Julius and Chris having got into another vital discussion at the front door. That had given Amy a chance to start clearing in the kitchen, and by the time Julius came to find her she had packed up anything she was taking home, and loaded the dishwasher.

'Leave that,' he said. 'You deserve a drink. You hardly drank anything all evening.'

Now that the guests had gone, she felt suddenly very nervous at the idea of being alone with Julius. She laughed a little awkwardly. 'That's very kind of you, but I wasn't here to enjoy myself, you know!'

The dark brows creased in a slight frown. 'Does that mean you *didn't* enjoy it?'

'Oh, yes, I did—very much.' She hadn't meant to sound critical. 'It's just that cooks have to keep their wits about them.'

She wasn't sure she had her wits about her now: there was something in the way he was looking at her that was making her very aware of him in a way she knew she shouldn't be. Not when he was engaged to Fiona.

She agreed, in the end, to accept a very small glass of brandy with a cup of coffee. They went back into the sitting-room, now lit only by one lamp, and she perched uncomfortably on the edge of a chair. Then she watched him as he picked up a heavy cut-glass decanter from the sideboard. The lamplight reflected golden from the surface of the glass, and she found herself looking at the long, lean fingers that held it. She glanced at his face—he was turned a little away from her, and she studied the clean-cut profile, with its straight nose and firm chin, and the line of his mouth . . . and she knew it was a mistake to have accepted the drink.

He sat at a little distance from her on the sofa, leaning back in a relaxed way that made her feel very stiff and formal. He started to talk casually about the Spanish deal, telling her more of the background to the venture while she wondered how soon she could decently drink her coffee and leave.

After a while she glanced very obviously at her watch.

'Julius, it's very late—I have to go.'

She didn't have to go, and she didn't want to. Charlie was staying the night at Celia's. She could have stayed and talked to Julius until dawn if he'd wanted her to. She got up, but before she could move away he was on his feet, standing in front of her. He put his hands on her arms.

'Amy, I really am grateful for what you did tonight.' His touch was sending signals all over her body. It was vital she get away before she made an idiot of herself.

This is stupid, she kept telling herself. I'll be behaving just like Zoe in a minute. She guessed what he was going to do. She didn't know whether to pull away, or just to let him kiss her and pretend it meant nothing—and that fractional indecision had consequences she could never have foreseen.

She didn't know what kind of kiss she was expecting—probably something that was not much more than a vague affectionate impulse on Julius's part. Maybe that was what had prompted him—she didn't know— but as soon as his lips touched hers, and he pulled her gently into his arms, something seemed to happen to her, despite all her wariness. His mouth on hers was soft at first, almost experimental, but a delicious feeling of warmth flooded through her, and without being fully conscious of what she was doing she put her arms round his neck.

His own arms tightened in response, and she instinctively pressed closer, moulding her body to the contours of his, letting her slim fingers slide up into that thick, short, silky hair she'd been longing to touch, encouraged by the reluctant groan that was torn from him. And then, at that precise moment, she realised just what all that confused antagonism she'd felt towards him had been about—since the very beginning. She must have been mad not to see it before—perhaps what she'd learned of him from Maxine had changed her perspective suddenly, but she knew now that all the unworthy motives she'd ascribed to him had just been a blind for herself, so that she wouldn't have to face an impossible truth.

And it was impossible, because it was sheer stupidity to let herself fall in love with a man who was already engaged to someone else.

That thought stabbed her with guilt—she must stop this—it was her fault because she was encouraging it... But she didn't want him to stop.

The kiss became more intense, his tongue exploring her mouth deeply as his lips moved on hers. It was as though that strange dream she'd had was suddenly becoming real—but so much more insistent and demanding than anything she could have imagined. She could feel his heartbeats quickening against her own. Then he broke off, releasing her to take her face in his hands.

'Amy...Amy...' he said her name unsteadily, his voice unexpectedly rough. She didn't know what he was trying to tell her—that he found her attractive, or that he didn't mean to let her get involved. But then he smiled, the corners of his mouth creasing in a way that made her want to kiss him again. 'Did you know you had freckles on your neck?' And his thumb caressed the edge of her jawline. 'I've been fascinated by them all evening.'

She ought to have pulled away from him then, and they could both have got out of it fairly gracefully, with no harm done to either of them. But perhaps, already, it was too late. For her, the harm had been making itself from that first day she had walked into his office.

He began to kiss her once more, his lips skimming down the side of her face to nuzzle the lobe of her ear. She could feel the sensuous glide of his tongue over her skin and she shivered while a heady kind of excitement flared within her. That this was she, Amy, who was too thin and who didn't eat enough and who got into trouble in the office for being inept...but for now he wasn't her boss, and she knew instinctively that she was the one with the power—the power of a woman's body over a man's, and against all common sense she let that sweet crazy exultation take her over just for a few intoxicating moments as she gave in to her desire to please him, to increase his desire for her, and to express, if only for this once, some of the secret attraction that had been there, even if she hadn't recognised it, from the first.

She was aware of his hand at the back of her waist, unfastening Fiona's belt, and that by slow steps he was walking her backwards. Then the belt came free, and was discarded, and as his hand slipped up over her bare skin underneath the tight black jersey top the back of her legs came into contact with the sofa and the slow reverse across the floor came to an abrupt halt. Then he was pulling her down with him, while the kiss renewed itself with greater intensity.

His weight on her, the hardness of his body pressed into her own was at once a surprising new reality and a further stimulus to desire. She was intensely aware of the heat of those muscled limbs under the light barrier of his clothing, and a delirious, almost frightening weakness began to pour through her, tingling through her limbs, softening, melting all resistance to him. One hand was under her back, but the other caressed the side of her slim waist, stroking, stealing up over her ribs, under the light stretchy lace of her bra, until involuntarily she arched against him with a quick indrawn breath. He shifted slightly, one thigh now lying between hers, and the hand that had been trapped under her now travelled quickly, in a light, tantalising caress, up one long leg, smoothing, exploring the contours of her thigh and hip with increasing intimacy.

They must stop now—they must!—or it would be too late.

She tried to tear her mouth from his, gasping, turning her face aside so that his lips were on her cheek, and then the line of her jaw.

'Julius—stop! Please——' Her voice was husky, almost hoarse, but her body seemed to be screaming its need of him. She didn't want him to stop—she wanted him to go on and on, to ease that ache that was beginning to build inside her—but her mind still insisted that nothing would be worth the regret they would both feel afterwards. 'We shouldn't be doing this—what about Fiona?'

He was very still suddenly. Then he shifted his weight a little from her, pushing himself up on one elbow to turn her face towards him with ungentle fingers.

'What about Charlie?' His voice sounded surprisingly harsh.

A little frown creased her brows, and she looked up into his eyes to find them unexpectedly hostile. 'What *about* Charlie?' she repeated dazedly.

'Charlie doesn't count but Fiona does, is that it?' He sounded angry—and in that instant she realised what that harmless little deception about Charlie had led to: with her live-in lover at home to go back to, in Julius's eyes she still wasn't averse to a bit of fun with the boss if he felt like it after a row with his girlfriend.

Seeing herself suddenly from his angle, she was appalled. She stared up into his eyes, her own an intense blue.

'No, Charlie doesn't count!' she said defiantly. 'Charlie is my fourteen-year-old brother!'

For a moment he looked completely taken aback. She tried to twist out from under him, but he wasn't prepared to let her go yet.

'So why did I believe he was your boyfriend?' he demanded. '*Look* at me, Amy!'

She met his furious glare. 'You jumped to that conclusion! I never said anything about him!'

'You let me believe it,' he argued. 'Why?'

She felt helplessly angry now. It was true, she couldn't deny it, but it was also true that she hadn't lied to him.

'Maybe I didn't care what you believed!' she flashed at him. 'My private life has nothing to do with you!'

There was another silence.

She felt him shift his weight, and then he was getting to his feet. She sat up quickly, pulling down her top and skirt.

'Since we're on the subject,' he said coldly, 'neither has my private life anything to do with your little mothers' meetings at the office. I'd be grateful if you didn't see fit to entertain the others with gossip about tonight.'

He must have a humiliatingly low opinion of her, and that hurt more than anything else. But if he could be cold, she was more than capable now of meeting ice with ice.

'That was unnecessary,' she said frigidly. 'I wouldn't dream of it. It's not of sufficient interest to me.'

She left soon after that. In silence, Julius helped her pack the boxes back into the car, and she collected her jeans and sweater from his bedroom.

How she managed to drive home safely she was never quite sure—tears of anger and humiliation blurred her vision far too often, as she thought of the way a successful evening had turned into a disastrous one.

She was very grateful that she had two whole days to herself before she had to face Julius again at the office.

CHAPTER FIVE

AMY wasted a lot of time over the weekend trying, unsuccessfully, to sort out her feelings. Once she'd got over her humiliation at the way Julius must have thought of her, she began to despise him for being a callous opportunist enjoying himself behind Fiona's back. Then she was forced to admit that her limited interpretation of events didn't fit all the evidence as neatly as she would have liked. Which was a pity; it would have been easier to go on resenting him.

She couldn't blame Julius, although she wanted to. Honesty forced her to admit that what had happened between them seemed to have taken him by surprise just as much as it had her. Maybe he had genuinely forgotten Fiona in those moments, or maybe he had never expected a harmless kiss to go so far, but either way he must have been surprised by her own response. Then, to be fair, when she had accused him of behaving badly towards Fiona, he had been quite justified—because of the way she had misled him over Charlie—in condemning her for a similar deception.

But she was still shattered by the way in which her own most primitive feelings had overwhelmed her with such unfamiliar intensity. Perhaps it was the fact that her life was so difficult at present that made her vulnerable to Julius's particular brand of charm, and concern, but she knew that if he had wanted her she'd have given herself to him, despite Fiona—despite everything. She despised herself for it, and couldn't make up her mind how much of her resentment against Julius was really anger with herself for her own weakness. She regretted now the way they had parted. She had provoked a childish row when, if she'd stopped to think about the way the misunderstanding over Charlie had caused Julius to react, she could perhaps have defused the situation, and they could have parted friends. Even if the kiss *had* been a mistake.

The office would be no place to make up a row like that. She would just have to be very cool on Monday, and as one-hundred-per-cent efficient as effort could make her. Then a rather chilling thought struck her—was he unscrupulous enough to sack her? She was still on trial at Prior Harding's. After what he would see as such an embarrassing little episode, he might easily look for the first excuse to get rid of her. And she was far from the ideal secretary!

She would have to make sure she gave him no cause for complaint, even comment. Then he would believe that what had happened had no real significance for her. That way, it could present no threat, and there would be no repercussions. But, despite her common-sense resolution, she spent all weekend thinking about him.

On Monday the post arrived unusually early. There was a large white envelope on the doormat, and the handwriting was unfamiliar.

She tore it open, half her mind, as usual at that time of the morning, on Charlie and the cat. There was a large, stiff double-sided invitation inside, and she had read it before she realised.

Mr and Mrs Anthony Harper-Maxwell invite Miss Amy Thompson to the wedding of their daughter Fiona to Mr Julius Prior on...

Her hands were shaking. Despite her rationalised approach to it all, she had been living since last night in two different worlds. In one world, she and Julius had just discovered a mutual attraction had taken them both by surprise—and in that private world outside the office and the claims of everyday life, somewhere below the level of conscious thought, she had been indulging in a sort of formless fantasy in which she cared for Julius, and he for her, in a way that made Fiona entirely irrelevant. Now one uncompromising white square of card reminded her that that world had been total illusion. In the real world there was Fiona, and there was the office, and her boss had kissed her in a way he shouldn't have done, as a result of which her job might be in jeopardy. And that was the reality she should have been living all the time.

She tore up the invitation and threw it away. She would make absolutely sure she was doing something that would guarantee acceptance impossible. It was only an office perk, and it wouldn't make any difference if she was there or not. She didn't know how she was going to get through the day at the office. Or face Julius. She found herself resenting him again.

Excited discussion of the invitations—both Zoe and Jacquie had received them—vied with minute analysis of hot news, courtesy of a friend of a friend of Jacquie's, that Fiona had been seen only that weekend at a dance in London wrapped round a handsome fair-haired man. Amy, mindful of Julius's parting comment, refused to be drawn into the gossip.

'I think for someone who's supposed to be getting married to our Julius, and with the wedding only weeks away, the beloved Fiona is behaving very badly!' Jacquie remarked, in a final attempt to get some interested reaction out of her. 'Something must have gone wrong. Has she met someone else—or has *he*?'

Amy stifled the inconvenient little fantasy that had revived again at the speculation, and gave a sweet and insincere smile. 'I can't imagine!' she said, and went back to concentrate ferociously on her typing.

Julius didn't come into the office on Monday, which was both a relief and a disappointment, and the following day he was so busy she scarcely saw him.

They never exchanged a word. The first time their paths crossed he gave her a sharp look, and then, later, a small sideways smile that despite all her resolutions she found rather endearing. Her own answering smile, though, was merely perfunctory. Whatever had happened in his flat was firmly in the past. Dennis's secretary could have nothing to do with the girl in the sexy black clothes who had cooked and served his dinner on Saturday night, sat with his friends, and then let him get within inches of seducing her.

Jess rang her when she got home to tell her that a cheque made out to Cookery Unlimited had arrived through the post. She had guessed from the signature the nature of the 'Abbott' mistake, but her excited demands for details of the evening were countered by Amy's heavily edited version. It was the first time she had ever been reluctant to discuss anything with her friend.

Why hadn't Julius taken an opportunity to give her the cheque in the office? It would have saved him trouble. But perhaps he preferred to avoid a direct encounter, and the inevitable uncomfortable reminder of what had happened between them.

'It's an awful lot more than we quoted!' Jess was exclaiming. 'Do you think he made a mistake?'

She felt suddenly cold. Julius didn't make mistakes about money. 'How much more?' she asked suspiciously.

'Well, not quite twice as much, but getting on that way. Could he have thought that the price we gave him was just for one cook, and he's paying us for two and deducting a bit because I wasn't there—if you see what I mean?'

'I don't think he was working it out on that basis.'

'So the extra's a tip? He must have liked you an awful lot!'

A tip. For services beyond the call of duty perhaps? But it hadn't been like that, and he knew it. Perhaps now, in the cold light of day, he was feeling guilty, and perhaps he'd seen Fiona since. Hush-money? Or an apology for the way the evening had ended?

It made her feel ashamed. And then angry. 'Jess, we're not going to accept it!'

Jess was incredulous at the other end of the phone. 'You must be mad! It wasn't a cheap dinner in the first place, but this is money way beyond our usual avarice!'

'I'm serious,' she insisted, suddenly feeling very tight inside. 'It's a mistake. Listen, bring the cheque round here tonight and I'll ask him about it in the office tomorrow. We should at least give him the chance to get it back.'

Her friend groaned. 'You're too honest.' But she couldn't really disagree.

No, Amy thought later, I'm not honest. I'm just cross—and hurt—that he thinks he can make a bad situation better by paying me for something that shouldn't have happened.

She dithered about her moment for confronting Julius. Stock market trading had a slow start, and neither he nor Dennis seemed to have much to occupy them. Finally, when Julius asked for coffee, she plucked up her courage and offered to act as waitress instead of Zoe, with the excuse that she wanted a signature on a letter. It would be the first time they had had an opportunity to speak to each other since Friday night.

Julius was just about to pick up the phone as she came in. He abandoned it, and sat back in his chair, playing with a pencil on the desk in front of him and eyeing her. She couldn't assess his mood.

'Yes, Amy. What can I do for you?'

Businesslike. Real life, she thought. And a tiny flickering hope she'd been nourishing despite herself that he might have made one favourable reference to Friday died instantly. She couldn't read his expression, although for Julius it seemed almost too carefully neutral.

She said, 'We can't accept this.' And put the cheque down with the coffee.

He glanced at it, and then looked back at her directly, his eyes piercing. 'Why not? Did I forget to sign it?'

He could see that he hadn't. And he could see that *she* could see that he hadn't.

'No,' she said awkwardly. 'But it's too much.'

'*Too much?*' Both dark eyebrows arched. 'What sort of business are you supposed to be running?'

'You know the job wasn't worth as much as this!' she replied defiantly.

'Do I? It was worth it to me. All right, then, consider the extra a tip.'

That was just what she'd been afraid of. 'For devotion beyond the call of duty?' She couldn't keep the sarcasm out of her voice and the phrase, particularly apt, was out before she meant it. She could see from the sudden flicker in his eyes that he understood exactly what she had been alluding to. She hadn't forgotten one smallest particle of a second of what had happened when he had begun to kiss her. She couldn't expect him to remember it exactly the way she did, but she could see now—she just knew—he hadn't forgotten it either.

'That has nothing to do with it,' he said abruptly. 'Why be so aggressive about it? I didn't take anything you didn't want to give—and we both know that.'

That had been true at the time, she couldn't deny it, but it didn't make it any better. And it wasn't particularly sensitive of him to point it out. It made her sound cheap.

She felt the blush creeping over her face, and knowing that she was blushing made it worse. 'I just don't want to be *paid* for it afterwards!'

He held the cheque delicately between two lean fingers of one hand, and looked down at it for a while. Then his eyes met hers, and there was a steely glint in them.

'I'm sorry if you think that. I was extremely grateful to you, Amy—I *am* grateful—for what you did on Friday night. You turned what could have been a difficult evening for me into a very enjoyable one. You did far more than you were required to by the terms of your employment because I asked you a favour, and I wanted to show you I really appreciated it. Why not go out and buy yourself and Jess a present?' His glance raked over her and he held out the offending cheque. 'And if you're stuck for ideas, why not start by buying yourself a pair of tights? You don't seem to do too well with them.'

The sarcasm wasn't too obvious from his tone, but it was there all right. She opened her mouth to explode, couldn't think of what to say exactly, shut it, and then took the cheque from his outstretched hand.

'I'm sure your partner will be able to bring herself to bank it, even if you can't.' There was a little more warmth in that, even a glint of humour, as though he was allowing himself to soften just a little. 'Was there anything else?'

Hating him for the way he was making fun of her, and embarrassed because she'd made a stupid issue over something he'd clearly dismissed as incidental—after all, she was the one who had claimed that his existence outside their work was a matter of indifference to her—she muttered a just audible, 'Thank you,' and got out of the office in record time. She had to admit that his words on the topic of Friday night had been appreciative, but too often he had a way of putting her in the wrong that made her look a complete fool. If only it weren't so desperate that she keep her job! she thought with some resentment. He wouldn't see her for dust—but only after she'd given him a very good idea of what she thought of him first!

It was outside the door that she remembered the letter she'd had for him to sign, still clutched in one hand. She couldn't bring herself to go back in again. She would have to ask his co-director for a signature later.

She avoided Julius for the rest of the day, paying the cheque into her joint account with Jess in the lunchhour, and ringing her when she got home that evening.

Charlie, surprisingly, didn't have any homework to do, but she didn't feel up to nagging him and collapsed in front of the television, using the images on the screen merely as a background to her thoughts. Deliberately, she avoided a replay of what had happened in the office and wondered instead, in a vague and inconstructive way, what she ought to do about preparations for Christmas.

Christmas Day itself they would be spending with Jess and her family. It would be the first Christmas since the deaths of their parents, and she was very anxious that she and Charlie shouldn't spend it alone. The contrast with the last one would be too stark.

She found herself thinking about the extra money Julius had given them. It was ironical that with all the expensive food she had to buy for the business she couldn't afford to feed Charlie in the way she would have liked. But she could buy a few small presents, more as jokes than anything else, and a Christmas tree—thanks to Julius, of course, though the last thing she wanted was to have to feel grateful to him just at the moment.

She fell asleep in front of the television set.

She didn't know whether her headache next morning was the result of the crick in her neck she'd got from

spending half the night so uncomfortably, or merely the
tension of the last few days making itself felt. And when
she wasn't expecting Julius to pounce on her for something she'd done wrong even the normal office routine
was a strain.

The headache, despite several doses of aspirin wasn't
going away, and her throat felt as though she'd swallowed
a knife. She felt very weird all over.

'You look awful!' Zoe told her cheerfully. 'Are you
sure you ought to be here?'

By that time she wasn't sure where she ought to be.
She couldn't understand why at the cottage, where there
was no heating, she'd felt OK, and here, in centrally
heated offices, she was shivering.

'Ask Dennis if you can go home,' Jacquie advised.
'You sound as though you're coming down with flu.'

Go home. That was the best thing anyone had said so
far! The wait for a bus was a daunting prospect, so it
would be better to ask Dennis now and get away as soon
as possible, especially if the flu she was suffering from
was one of those lightning-strike varieties.

But it wasn't Dennis, with his friendly concern, she
encountered first—it was Julius, whose rather abrasive
manner made his response sound more like an accusation than a solicitous enquiry.

'What on earth's the matter with you?' he demanded,
giving her one of those laser looks. 'You're always a bit
pale but now you look positively ghastly. You shouldn't
have come in to work.'

Because she might infect the rest of the office? It was
difficult even to summon up the energy to answer him,
and she found herself mumbling, 'I'll be fine if I can go
now.'

'How are you getting back home?'

'Bus.'

She wasn't sure now whether she was answering him or not—it was such an effort to get a word out, and it seemed important not to let him see how much she was shivering. He looked unreal, his body remote but somehow threatening, and she was only aware of his eyes—their colour and the intensity of their gaze. She hadn't the strength to face any fuss. If only they would all leave her alone to get the bus home in peace!

He said something she didn't catch, and then Jacquie was helping her on with her coat. She was hardly conscious of collecting her things together, although she was aware that she was leaving a letter half typed. She started to try to explain about it.

'Don't worry about that. I'll finish it for you,' Jacquie offered kindly. 'Come downstairs with me. I'll help you. He's gone to get the car.'

What car? It wasn't running. It had been parked in Mr Watson's drive for the last four months!

The staircase seemed to sway round her as she made her way downstairs, and the feel of Jacquie's fingers gripping her arm were the only reality. She felt truly awful.

The cold fresh air of the street was momentarily reviving. Jacquie stood with her on the pavement until the grey Mercedes pulled up alongside the kerb and Julius got out, leaving the engine running.

Without knowing quite how she got there, she found herself sitting in the passenger seat, leaning her head back against the head-rest, her eyes closed. The headache was no better, and she was floating in an unreal world, but at least she didn't have to make an effort to stand. She was still inexplicably cold.

She was aware that Julius had got in beside her, without saying anything. She wondered dazedly where they were going, her thoughts becoming deliriously confused. Perhaps he would use this as an excuse to get rid of her?

Then after a while he was saying suddenly, 'This is Applecot. Which is your house? Amy?'

She opened her eyes. He was sitting sideways in the car looking at her, a frown creased between his dark brows. 'Amy—are you awake?'

She pulled herself together. They were in the main street.

'Turn right at the end,' she muttered vaguely.

'Here?'

'Mm.'

They were parked in the middle of the row of cottages. 'Which house?'

'The one at the end.' It took all her effort to get that out. The rest he would have to guess.

The car had stopped again. He reached forward to open the handbag in her lap, and picked out a bunch of keys.

He held them up. 'These?'

She nodded. He got out, and with the part of her mind that was vaguely rational she expected him to come round immediately to the passenger door, but when he did reappear it was without the keys. He opened the door.

'Come on, not much more. Swing your legs out. That's right. Now—let me pull you up.'

Before she was conscious of obeying any of his curt instructions, she suddenly felt herself being lifted up. Strong arms round her back and under her knees.

'Put your arm round my neck——'

She rested her head against a shoulder. It was wonderfully reassuring, comforting. She wished she didn't feel so utterly ill.

Julius carried her up the path to the front door, which was open, and into the hall; then he was taking her upstairs. She clung to him and shut her eyes. He seemed to know without asking which door opened into her bedroom.

He put her down on the bed, and looked at her.

'There's a young man with spiky red hair downstairs who says he's your brother. Do I believe him?'

Charlie? What was he doing...? He should be at school——

'Get into bed. It's damn cold in here.'

'There's an electric fire downstairs.' She thought she said the words, but she wasn't sure if they came out right.

He left her lying on the bed, wondering if she ought to get undressed, and feeling too ill to move. But it was better lying down. She didn't know if she'd find the strength ever to get up again.

It seemed a very long time before he reappeared, Charlie behind him clutching the electric fire.

Charlie shouldn't be there.

She managed to croak, 'What are you doing home from school?'

He looked sheepish. 'I—er—didn't feel too well.'

'You look just fine to me,' Julius said harshly. 'It's your sister who's ill, not you. Are you going to help her get undressed or shall I?'

With the bit of her brain that was still functioning, she thought that if she'd felt better she'd have been amused by the expression of undisguised dismay that crossed her brother's face. He vanished from the room with the speed of light.

In other circumstances, she would have got a secret pleasure out of being undressed by Julius, but feeling as she did there was nothing particularly pleasurable about the touch of his hands—she ached all over, and was conscious only that he was stripping her down to her underwear with clinical efficiency. She didn't even care that her underwear was distinctly ragged at the edges, and she had a safety pin in one of the straps of her bra. She felt too ill to be embarrassed by it.

She became aware that he had been standing looking down at her as she lay on the bed. She stared up at him, her eyes meeting his, but she couldn't read any of the thoughts behind that extraordinary lucid gaze. Then his expression became shuttered, and with a deft twitch he pulled the duvet over her.

'Are you going to be all right on your own—is there anyone I can ring? Your friend Jess?'

'I'm OK,' she managed to say. 'There's Charlie.'

'Ah. Charlie.'

That sounded somehow significant, but she couldn't guess what it meant. She was too ill to care. Under the comforting warmth of the duvet, she was grateful to be allowed to slip into a semi-conscious doze.

It could have been minutes or hours later when she became aware of her brother standing at her bedside, a glass of something in his hand. 'He says to drink this.'

'Who?' It was an effort to pull her thoughts together.

'Julius. Your boss. He took me to the chemist's in the village. He says you've probably got flu and if you're any worse tomorrow I've got to ring the doctor.'

She thought about the information. The facts kept sliding apart so that they didn't make any real sense to her. 'Where is he?'

'Gone to a meeting, he said.'

It was silly to wish it, but she wanted him to come back. She felt very much alone. There was something she had to remember, something she had to say to Charlie. She drank the stuff in the glass. It had a bitter taste like aspirin. Perhaps she'd think of what she wanted to say later.

Later. Much later, she woke up. She didn't feel any better, but her mind was a bit clearer, with one extra-ordinary thought in it—Julius had brought her home!

It seemed like a dream now, but he had actually carried her upstairs and undressed her...

'Charlie?'

Spiked ginger hair and a freckled face appeared round the door.

'Ring Jess for me and tell her I've got flu? If you speak to her nicely she might even be persuaded to come round and open a can of baked beans for you.'

'It's OK,' he replied offhandedly. 'I can do that.'

'Well, ring her anyway.' She hesitated, and then asked, 'Did Julius drive you back from the chemist's?'

'Yeah.'

He really had gone out of his way to help her. She remembered Maxine's comment about his kindness. But with so many conflicting impressions it was hard to know what she should really think of him. She shut her eyes. 'You were a lot of use when he brought me in here.' She tried to sound sarcastic. 'He could have been a total stranger who'd picked me up on the way home for all the trouble you took to find out about him. Supposing he'd decided to rape me? I like the way you ran away the minute he suggested taking my clothes off!'

'He looked as though he might have had practice at it,' her brother suggested awkwardly. 'Anyway, I'd have been around. He knew who I was and he wanted to know what I was doing home from school.'

She waited. 'And...?'

'I just didn't feel too well. I didn't want to bother you at the office.'

She looked at him. She could tell when Charlie was lying. His eyes, a paler blue than her own, always took on a particularly glassy expression. Just like now. She was surprised he'd brought up the topic at all—perhaps he wanted to get the subject out of the way when he knew she didn't have strength to pursue it.

Then her heart sank. She still hadn't fully taken in yet the fact that Julius had brought her home, and she certainly hadn't had time to work out all the implications of it, but one thing was clear—it was a pity he'd ever had to meet Charlie. He was far too astute to be taken in by any of her brother's prevarications. And if there was one thing she couldn't afford to let him know about it was home problems. He had once asked her to confide in him, but that was before the disastrous events at his flat after the dinner party. To let him know there were any difficulties with Charlie now would be like handing him on a plate the perfect excuse to get rid of her! Whatever her private and very mixed feelings about her boss, she couldn't afford to jeopardise her job, for *any* reason.

'Ring Jess, there's a good brother,' she said weakly.

CHAPTER SIX

AMY was in bed for two days. Charlie's call to the Baileys brought both Jess and her mother round to see her separately, twice, and she felt an overwhelming relief at the sight of Celia. Jess's mother was someone towards whom she could feel uncomplicated gratitude, whereas in the case of Julius the situation was far from being so straightforward. Would he have done as much for Zoe or Jacquie? No, she had to admit it to herself, he would not. So why exactly, when he seemed to have made it clear she was just an office girl once more, had he gone out of his way to help her?

Common sense warned her not to indulge any further in idle fantasies. Julius was engaged to Fiona. Nothing changed that.

Sunday was cold and wet, but she got up anyway. The prospect of staying at home alone once Charlie was at school on Monday was dismal. She decided to go back to work despite mixed feelings about her next confrontation with Julius. All her determination to keep her worlds separate had come to nothing now her boss had had such a detailed view of her own private affairs—and just how detailed emerged from a conversation with Charlie.

'He had a pretty good look round the house,' he told her, after an attempt to elicit from him exactly how far Julius had put himself out for her when he had brought her home. 'He seemed to think the whole place needed re-wiring!'

She looked at him aghast. 'How did he find that out?' Perhaps she'd been delirious, and time had passed very differently from the way she'd imagined?

Her brother gave a dismissive shrug. 'The electric fire wasn't working. He went on a hunt for the spare fuses.'

It was true, there *had* been rather a long wait before they had brought up the fire to her bedroom. But the thought of Julius inspecting her shabby sitting-room and spartan kitchen, making a mental inventory of her inadequate housekeeping, was humiliating in the extreme!

Julius wasn't in when she arrived at the office on Monday, and she was on edge the whole morning, wondering when he would appear. She willingly agreed to hold the fort while the other two secretaries went out for lunch together—it would be easier to see him without an audience. Any reference, however cryptic, to events at Number 5 Estate Cottages could fuel office gossip for weeks.

Poring over her word processor in the reception area, she was unaware of his arrival, and his brisk greeting nearly made her jump out of her skin.

'Well, Amy. How do you feel now? You were like a limp rag when I took you home the other day!'

Faced very suddenly with nearly six feet of Julius's particular brand of dynamic attraction and only the width of her desk between them, she was acutely conscious that the last time they had been together he had been undressing her in her own bedroom—and he'd seen her awful underwear... She pushed an untidy strand of hair behind her ear in an awkward gesture.

'I'm fine—much better——' She wasn't quite sure how to go on.

His eyes caught hers for a moment, and from the spark in them she just knew he was thinking about that safety pin. Her heart seemed to be jumping up and down far too fast.

'Judging by today's picture of blooming health, I don't have to feel too bad about not getting round to see you with the grapes, then?'

She gave a grin, meeting his eyes again. 'I like them better as wine anyway!'

His expression gave nothing away, except a kind of superficial amusement, but somehow she felt sure that underneath he was wound up for something. Was he busy collating computer-fashion all the information he'd got in that brief visit to the cottage, and preparing to announce the end of her very short spell of employment at Prior's? *Home problems*. Surely he must have enough evidence by now that she was in no way the secretary he wanted?

'Charlie been looking after you properly?'

'He was very helpful.' It sounded a bit weak, but she didn't want to explore that particular subject.

'Did you find out what he was doing at home the day I brought you back from the office?'

Again she hedged. 'He—he didn't feel too well. He didn't want to worry me at work.'

She definitely didn't like the look he gave her at that— the 'laser look', as Jacquie called it.

'Really? That's not what he told me.'

Help! They were into the danger zone already. Trust Julius—probing for the weak spot before going in for the kill! She was forced to ask, 'What *did* he tell you?'

'That he'd forgotten a physics book, and had a lift home from one of the teachers on her half-day so that he could get it in his lunch-hour.'

Oh, Charlie! 'I'm sure it was perfectly innocent,' she lied quickly.

Julius was still looking at her. 'I'm not. You're not a fool, Amy,' he said shortly. 'You must have guessed he's skiving off somewhere. You can't afford to ignore it—

he could get into serious trouble. You'll be getting a call from the school if it goes on.'

She lifted her chin and stared at him defiantly this time. 'It's nothing I can't handle!' Now sack me! she thought. You're the one who's saying I've got problems, not me!

There was an unexpected pause before the laser look took on a different glint. Perhaps he'd remembered she'd just been ill. 'Amy the mother,' he commented. 'A long way from the Amys I know.'

She was on the defensive again. 'What do you mean—Amys?'

His eyes held hers. 'Amy the secretary and Amy the siren.'

There was another loaded silence. Was this it at last, what he'd been getting round to, and all because of that wretched dinner party he was going to tell her he no longer thought it was a good idea for her to go on working at Prior's?

Nervousness made her reply unintentionally aggressive. 'I wasn't trying to seduce you that night!'

'I know that,' he said shortly. 'I didn't think I was trying to seduce you either. I never meant it to happen like that. Life has a way of taking you by surprise. Sometimes when you think you've got everything nicely worked out you find you haven't.'

His eyes held hers again briefly, but he obviously didn't intend to clarify that statement, turning on his heel towards his office. Then the phone rang.

'Switch it through, will you?' It was boss to secretary again. She let out a long, controlled sigh. He hadn't sacked her yet, anyway!

It was the last she saw of him for the rest of the day. She felt she'd had a lucky escape from a discussion she wasn't sure she'd fully understood. She pondered Maxine's words, about computer programs, and the way

Julius ran his life. The gist of the message he'd just given her seemed to be that even though the after-dinner episode hadn't featured in his program he had now filed it away as simply that: an episode.

But what it didn't explain very satisfactorily was the highly charged atmosphere that still remained between them. His 'filing away' the subject should have defused the situation once and for all, but it hadn't. She couldn't define what it was precisely, though some sixth sense told her that her increasing awareness of him was far from one-sided.

Then it was only a couple of days later that the curious tension that seemed to be winding itself up between them tightened again.

She was in his office, taking down instructions about a client, when Zoe buzzed on the telephone. Halfway into a sentence, Julius snatched up the receiver. She glanced up under her eyelashes, and found him looking directly at her. It wasn't difficult to deduce from the audible snatches of Zoe's message—and from his expression—that the call must be for her.

'Staff don't have time to take personal calls in working hours. Find out who it is, will you?' The cutting edge in his voice told her she'd just notched up another indelibly black mark, and she was wondering whether it was worth making general apologies to soften him a bit, or whether it was Jess with an emergency and she should just insist on taking it, when Zoe buzzed back and the words 'headmaster' and 'school' were all too clear.

Julius gave her one of those piercing looks, and her heart dropped like a stone. Truancy—it had to be. The very last thing she wanted to hear. And he couldn't say he hadn't warned her.

'She can take it in here,' he instructed curtly, then he held out the receiver to her.

She stood up hastily. 'It's OK—I'll go through to Recep——'

He didn't give her a chance to finish, thrusting the receiver into her hand. 'You'd better talk to him.'

She wondered even while they talked whether Julius could hear Mr Parry's contribution to the conversation. She tried to keep her replies to an enigmatic minimum, conscious all the time of Julius busily scribbling a memo at the other side of the desk. He didn't appear to be paying the slightest attention—but she'd learned to mistrust that. When she finally put the receiver down carefully, she stared at her notepad, hoping he would resume where he'd left off. She knew he wouldn't.

He leaned back in his chair and looked at her very directly. 'So what did Mr Parry have to say?'

'It was nothing,' she said airily. 'Just a call to find out if Charlie was all right, so I said it was he who had been ill and not me—I didn't know how they'd react to the idea of one of their pupils staying at home to look after his sister.'

He gave her one long, mind-numbing look. 'Don't take me for an idiot, Amy! No headmaster of a school the size of Charlie's has time to make polite calls in the middle of the day. Charlie's cut school again today—and yesterday?'

'If you heard so much of the conversation, why are you asking me?' she said defensively. It was bad enough to be rung up in the first place, without Julius becoming involved.

'I'd like to hear your version of it, that's all.'

'I'm not accountable to you!' she flashed, unguardedly, her eyes suddenly very blue. 'You're making it sound as though I'm the one playing truant—not Charlie! My job here shouldn't have to depend on my brother's good behaviour in my private life—you're not being fair!'

Julius's own eyes took on a dangerous glint. 'Don't be ridiculous! Of course you're not accountable to me—it's your business and you can keep it that way if you want to, but I'm trying to help you. With advice if nothing else. I have a nephew Charlie's age who's not getting on too well at school either—maybe some joint action would be effective here.'

Oh, no, it wouldn't! That was a disastrous idea! Again it wasn't treating her as just an employee and she made up her mind on the spot that she couldn't afford to have her emotions shredded by him any further. But if she wasn't careful they would be having a blazing row, and then he probably would sack her.

She tried a different tack, running through a downbeat and highly edited version of the battle over school. The actual frequency of her brother's absences—not discussed openly with Mr Parry—and his suspected alternative amusements were left out.

'I can't blame Charlie,' she finished dismissively. 'He was at a private school until the end of last summer term. There was no more money to pay the fees, so he's had to go to this local comprehensive. It's good, but he's lost all his old friends, and I don't think he's really come to terms with what happened to Mum and Dad.' Then she added for good measure, 'There's no real problem.'

Julius leaned back in his chair abruptly. 'Of course there's a problem!' he retorted. 'And your behaving like an ostrich isn't going to solve anything——'

What could she say to that except, yet again, It's none of your business? Irritated, she bit her lip. He was making her out to look a fool.

'Your brother's at the very worst age now. He could go off the rails completely. You need someone with a bit of authority to deal with him.'

'And I've got none, you mean?'

He gave an impatient shrug. 'With the best will in the world, you can't take the place of his father. Look at the facts sensibly and don't get so touchy about it.'

He was telling her nothing new, but it was hard to swallow coming from him. He didn't wait for her comment, though. 'My sister's family are living in my house down in Wiltshire at the moment—they're in the process of moving, and they haven't got full possession of the new property yet. My nephew Ben and Charlie might get on very well.'

'So what? There's no guarantee it'll turn them both into models of virtue at school!' She couldn't help feeling piqued at the idea that Julius only had to step in and Charlie would be a reformed character, whereas she'd got no thanks for struggling with an impossible situation for months.

He gave her a piercing look. 'If you sit back and do nothing, the only thing you can guarantee is disaster! This way, it'd be good for Ben too—he's another one at a bit of a loose end at the moment.'

'There isn't an easy solution to this.'

'No, there isn't,' he agreed unexpectedly. 'And if there's one thing I'm beginning to learn it's that you can't count on nice neat businesslike plans when it comes to people. Life has a way of messing up all the most logical and sensible arrangements one makes.' From the way he was looking at her, she had a feeling there was more to that statement than was obvious from the context, but he went on, 'In the case of your brother, it's not going to do any harm to try.'

It was a statement, not even a pretence at seeking her agreement, and the finality of his tone signalled the end of the discussion. It left her feeling resentful; she was trapped. If she ignored his advice again and things went badly wrong, she couldn't expect much tolerance over the subsequent difficulties at work. He *would* sack her then—no question of it!

Once back home, she couldn't any longer avoid a confrontation with Charlie on the subject of truancy. She could see that with every word she said she was antagonising him.

'But it was only a couple of times!'

She sighed impatiently. She was getting nowhere. 'Only a couple of times a week, you mean! This is serious, Charlie! How do you think I feel being rung up at the office by your headmaster and having to pretend to my boss that it was just to pass the time of day? Honestly, you could have got me the sack, and then we wouldn't even have a roof over our heads!'

Her brother's face had that closed, sullen look. She tried a new angle. 'Look, Charlie, I know Julius seems a friendly and amusing guy to you, but he's hell to work for most of the time and my job depends on not having any problems with irate headmasters!'

Calling Mr Parry 'irate' was overstating it, but she could remember only too vividly that horrible sinking feeling she'd had when she'd heard who was on the other end of the line.

Her brother's expression didn't change. He got up abruptly.

'OK,' he said, without looking at her, and left the room.

She sighed again. What did 'OK' mean, for heaven's sake? OK I won't do it again? Or OK I've listened to you, now stop moaning at me? Which was no guarantee of anything.

Julius wasn't a man to waste any time once he'd made his mind up about something, but she was surprised, and rather annoyed, to discover from Charlie only a day later that he had been invited by her boss to spend Saturday with his nephew. Julius had rung him when he got home from school. He would collect him from Applecot after breakfast and deliver him back late on Saturday evening.

'I don't remember being consulted about this!' she began—and then relented. It wasn't fair to take it out on her brother. She *had* been consulted—by Julius, if his having made a unilateral decision on the subject counted as a consultation. She had to admit he had talked sense, and there was a chance the new contact might be good for Charlie.

When Saturday came she didn't even have a chance to say hello. Charlie, ready and waiting, had been out at the car before she'd had time to get to the front door, but Julius had merely given her a wave, before the Mercedes disappeared down the lane between the spiky winter hedges.

She looked doubtfully at the cat. 'Well, Rasputin. What do you think of that? Do I get the impression he's avoiding me? He could have waited!'

He didn't wait to talk when he brought her brother back, either, merely dropping him at the gate.

'He says sorry he can't stop but he's got to get back to the flat.'

'Oh,' she said. 'Nothing else?'

'To say hi or something.'

Or something. But what, exactly? His arrangements with Charlie now seemed to be excluding her completely!

Charlie's initial report on the day's entertainment was that it was 'brill', and by degrees she got out of him details of an enviable lifestyle involving horses, stables, hot-air balloons, wine-making in the cellars, and a cast of characters—nephew, niece, sister, brother-in-law— that made up Julius's home world. Including Fiona.

She felt a twinge of jealousy at that, though Charlie's comments on her were not complimentary. 'A bit of a pain,' he summed her up, and added the information that she and Julius had had a row.

The glimpse into Julius's private world was fascinating, but it hurt too, because it reminded her just how much a part of it Fiona was. Perhaps she shouldn't have torn up that wedding invitation. She should have kept it as a salutary reminder that any sort of idle dreaming about her boss was only going to make her unhappy in the end.

She would have to be very careful. It was sometimes hard not to show him that she had an interest in him beyond what was appropriate to her situation as a grateful employee. Of course, she didn't want to have to be grateful to him, but she hadn't much choice. She thought again of Maxine's comments about him. He'd probably run her through his mental computer in a file called 'Amy—problems' and the answer had come back as 'generally in need of assistance'. She told herself she ought to feel pleased that now he knew a little more about her situation he was interested in helping her. He'd accepted the fact that she was running her own business in addition to her work at the office, and if the Charlie problems could be glossed over and her brother kept out of any real trouble she might be all right until she and Jess could finally devote themselves to Cookery Unlimited full-time. But it had landed her in a perpetual conflict of emotions—the strong attraction that didn't seem to be getting any weaker, no matter how severely she tried to control it, warring with the humiliating feeling that he'd adopted her as his 'good cause'!

Seeing him in the office again on Monday marked a further change. He was into a double dose of that bristling dynamic energy she could have done without. He had given her one of those 'now you see it, now you don't' smiles as he strode through the reception area, following it with a curt instruction to get one of his City contacts on the phone, and immediately vanished into his office. She reflected rather crossly that she was back in the 'inadequate secretary' pigeon-hole once more; he would only notice her when things went wrong and he wondered again about sacking her.

The office 'weather forecast' initially estimated him at 'fair', but as the morning wore on it became obvious that that was giving way to a stormy frame of mind which didn't seem to have much to do with work. A couple of unsuccessful phone calls didn't usually have him on the hop, and as far as they could judge trading was fairly steady on the Stock Exchange.

His mood hadn't improved the following day. He appeared to be on a remarkably short fuse.

'I want that done by three o'clock.'

The crisp instruction was also a dismissal.

She looked down at the document in her hand. 'But——'

'No *buts*, Amy.' His eyes met hers.

'I'll have to leave the——'

'I don't care what you leave,' he interrupted brusquely. 'Just get on with it.'

It was a measure of her suppressed feelings about him that she could no longer shrug off a remark like that—now she took it personally, and it hurt.

'It's probably Fiona problems,' Jacquie muttered as she passed on the way to her desk. 'No phone calls, no office visits from her for the last three weeks—what do we suspect? We suspect that *someone*—a certain fair-haired gentleman—has just sabotaged the wedding plans. The formidable Mrs H-M wouldn't be very pleased!'

Amy didn't comment, but thought of what Charlie had told her. His allusion to the row seemed to back up office interpretations.

Julius was going to be away from the office for the last couple of days before Christmas—two more days closer to the wedding she didn't want to think about. She tried to tell herself she was no better than Zoe, with a romantic crush on her boss because he was handsome and dynamic and sometimes teased her, but it wasn't any use—because he was already so much more than that.

The only real bonus for her as a result of Julius's absence would be the more relaxed atmosphere in the office. But given the choice she would far rather have his presence. There was a sort of dangerous sparkle in the air when he was around; when he was out the job became dull routine.

Her preparations for Christmas were rather haphazard. She brought a tree home from Wychford on the bus. Along with it had come a bargain offer of a bundle of holly, and an anaemic-looking sprig of mistletoe which she hung up in the porch rather than waste. But, apart from buying in some stock for a cooking job she and Jess had on Christmas Eve, the rest of the shopping would have to wait until the office cat was finally out of the way, and the mice would have an opportunity to extend their lunch-hours.

When the doorbell rang on Sunday evening, she thought at once that it must be Charlie without his key, back unexpectedly early from watching a video at Celia's. She'd been preparing to indulge in her usual end-of-the-week lassitude. She'd washed her hair and swathed it in a towel, from which the long dark red strands escaped untidily.

Shock for a moment deprived her of all speech. The very last person she might have expected to see—and there he was, on her doorstep!

'Julius!'

Had he made some arrangement with Charlie?

He was wearing an expensive leather jacket and jeans, but even casual clothes didn't make him look any less

the office tycoon—she sensed something wound-up,
businesslike, just in the way he stood there. His eyes
instantly took in the towel, the grey sweatshirt with its
Snoopy cartoon in dayglo pink borrowed from Charlie,
the tracksuit bottoms, and the inevitable football socks...
With all the wistful passion of a Cinderella, she wished
then—despite her resolutions to do nothing that would
suggest she had the faintest personal interest in him—
that once, just *once*, he could see her really glamorously
dressed!

'Aren't you going to ask me in?' he said, looking down
at her in a way that made her knees suddenly go weak.
'Or are you on your way out for an evening's
goalkeeping practice?'

She seemed to have lost her voice. 'I—yes—Charlie's
not here——'

'I haven't come to see your brother. I've come to see
you.'

'Social or strictly business?'

She tried to sound flippant to disguise the nerves or
whatever they were fluttering away inside her. It wasn't
just that he had caught her at a disadvantage—she felt
intensely aware of him. In the office there were secretaries, word processors, telephones to put between them.
Now there was nothing.

His face relaxed briefly into lines that creased the sides
of his mouth, and there was a spark in his eyes that
belied his next words. 'Strictly business!'

'Professional advice on the rewiring?' She
remembered what Charlie had said about his last visit.
He laughed, and stepped forward into the small hallway,
and she stood back to let him pass. She saw him notice
the mistletoe, but he didn't comment. His clothes smelled
of the cold night air, fresh and invigorating. She wondered if she should offer to take his coat.

He eyed the towel turban again. 'Sorry—I should have rung you.' He didn't sound in the least apologetic. 'I've got a business proposition to discuss with you.'

It sounded depressingly formal. She took his jacket, careful as always that her fingers shouldn't touch his, and stood wondering whether she ought to hang it up on the pegs in the same untidy manner as hers and Charlie's. He had his own coat-hanger at work. He read her indecision, and sounded amused. 'You don't have to give it special treatment, you know, Amy! We're not in the office now.'

She smiled, her eyes avoiding his this time. 'So you mean you lead a double life?' she joked, trying to dispel some of the awkwardness she felt.

'I'm beginning to think I do.'

It wasn't the answer she expected. Startled, she met his eyes directly. He was looking at her in a way she couldn't interpret, and his words had been unmistakably double-edged. She'd spent so long trying to suppress the hope that the attraction might, despite everything, be mutual, she couldn't now afford to believe what a sudden crazy suspicion told her he might be saying. But *surely* he couldn't be, after he had been virtually ignoring her for the past week?

Terrified of making a fool of herself if she'd guessed wrong, she asked stiffly, 'Would you like something to drink? It's only tea or coffee, I'm afraid.'

'Don't make anything specially. I can't stay long.'

She wasn't intending to have a drink, but it seemed like a good idea now. It would give her something to do while she gathered her wits together. 'I was just going to get a cup of tea.'

He followed her into the kitchen, and she felt as though every nerve-end was aware of him. In that confined space the air seemed to charge instantly with his own particular brand of energy. He put down the carrier bag he'd brought in with him on one of the surfaces.

'I've brought you and Charlie a Christmas present— Charlie's is outside in the car. This is for you.'

She didn't know what to say, the gesture was so unexpected. She looked in the carrier. It contained a bottle of wine. 'Julius!' The château label was a famous one. 'What—why are you giving me a present?' This is stunningly expensive! she thought, in embarrassed confusion.

'In lieu of the invalid's grapes—you said you'd prefer to drink them.'

'But I'm better now!'

'OK, then take it as standard office Christmas handout. You said when you came to dinner the other night you liked good wine.'

But she didn't want him to get away with a remark like that—it gave her no clues. 'I didn't come to dinner that night—I came to cook for you!'

The unusual grey eyes with their dark-ringed irises met hers, but the look he gave her was again disappointingly enigmatic. 'If that's the way you want to see it.' He changed the subject abruptly. 'I'll unload Charlie's Christmas present now, if you don't mind. Is there anywhere you can stack logs?'

'It's very kind of you to give us all this.' She couldn't help sounding doubtful. Ought she to accept it? 'Surely you don't do it for Zoe's brothers and sisters, and Jacquie's grandma as well?'

He glanced at her, and smiled, his eyes suddenly lighting with genuine humour in just the way that sparked a response deep inside her despite her reservations. 'Not the family extras, no—but then as far as I'm aware Jacquie's grandma isn't a potential delinquent! Anyway, I couldn't live with the thought of Charlie spending

Christmas scouring the countryside for fir-cones, which he assured me was going to be his fate.'

'So all this is Charlie's fault?' She laughed too, but awkwardly. She was secretly appalled at the thought of what her brother might have been telling the man who was her employer. She remembered how she'd made a joke to herself about busking in shopping centres. But there were ways and ways of begging!

His criticism of her fuel shed went some way to restoring that healthy antagonism that kept things in perspective. It was, according to him, badly stacked—Charlie's work; he'd piled her last load of logs under a leak in the roof—and he insisted on bringing a great deal of damp wood into the kitchen, where it took up most of the available floor space and shed woodlice on to the tiles.

'You'll never have a decent fire if you don't dry it out,' he told her impatiently. 'It's just a waste. This stuff looks as though you've excavated it from a local swamp.'

Why did she always get the feeling that he regarded her as totally inept when it came to practical matters?

'I stack the new wood by the fire!' she argued. 'That dries it perfectly!'

'Yes. In quantities ideal for the average doll's house.'

'I can only afford to heat the average doll's house!'

He gave her a sharp look at that, but didn't reply.

She'd made the tea while some of the unloading had been going on, and now she took it into the sitting-room. The fire was already laid, but unlit for economy reasons. The towel that swathed her hair fell down twice while she was lighting it. She was aware of Julius watching her. The look in his eyes disconcerted her—it could only be described as appraisal.

There was a pause, and it was while she pulled the towel away completely, letting her hair fall in long strands round her shoulders, that he said unexpectedly, 'You're an extraordinary woman, Amy—no one else I know could wear such dreadful clothes and still look such a siren.'

His expression gave her no clues, and she didn't know how to react—she *had* to be mistaken—'siren' was the word he'd used in an allusion to what had happened that night at his flat! How could he describe her like that now, dressed as she was in her awful clothes with hair that must look like wet red string? He couldn't really be telling her he still found her so attractive!

If only Charlie would come home! When he was around, this couldn't happen. If it *was* happening. But his next words didn't seem very serious, and then she wondered if he was trying to defuse some of the peculiar tension that seemed to be building up.

'Lighting fires and boiling kettles—I suppose it is appropriate to a witch after all.' 'Witch' evoked an image very different from 'siren'. She felt relieved—and a little disappointed. 'And what about those other skills you're supposed to have,' he went on, 'like telling my future? You promised me a tea-leaf consultation, remember?'

'That was your idea,' she protested quickly.

'Come on—don't tell me you don't know how to do it!'

'We've got tea-bags.'

'That shouldn't deter someone like you.'

What did he mean by that? On impulse, she got up, and standing in front of him gingerly took his empty cup. She pretended to glance into it, and then, without stopping to analyse what was prompting her, said rather quickly, 'I can see a ring—perhaps two rings. And a lot of people in a church—and a journey. And I'm sure you'll live happily ever after!'

There was an awful pause.

She didn't know why she'd let herself say it. It was about as strong a message as she could give that he had

no business to be making such ambiguous comments—
flirting with her even, if that was what he was doing.

She wished he would say something. She couldn't look
at him. That had been a stupid thing to say—it let him
know very clearly the trend of her thoughts, when she
had probably misread the situation completely. After
what seemed an age, he stretched out and took the cup
from her fingers, putting it on a low table.

'OK,' he said quietly, but there was a definite edge to
his voice now that told her her words had gone home.
The temperature of the room seemed to have dropped
several degrees. 'Now let me tell you *your* immediate
future——'

Her heart gave an ominous thud.

'Julius—I——' She ought to apologise before it got
any worse.

'You're going to get an offer.' He ignored her interruption, sounding suddenly cool and businesslike—as
though he were interviewing her all over again. 'It's an
offer you should accept. It leads to money, and foreign
travel.'

She frowned. It wasn't what she'd expected.

'What . . . exactly is the offer?' She went back to her
armchair and sat down. She felt too vulnerable standing
there in front of him.

His eyes held hers, their expression remote. 'A perfectly respectable one,' he said casually. 'I need a cook.
I've got a four-day trip to Spain at the beginning of
January. You've already dealt with some of the relevant
correspondence, and you know we've been able to
finance the purchase of more building land in the Puerto
Banus area near Marbella—thanks to Chris and others.
We're building some luxury houses there. I've been approached by Spanish property dealers about advance
sales of some of the projected buildings—which would
of course help to finance further stages of the devel-

opment. I need to go out there to help them make up their minds about us.'

She wasn't absolutely sure what he was leading up to. She wished he wouldn't look at her like that. She began to comb some of the tangles out of her hair with her fingers. It made her nervous just to sit there and do nothing.

His eyes assessed her, looking for her reaction.

'I want you to come down to the development with me and help entertain them.'

She was silent, unsure whether she'd heard him rightly. Go to Spain...in January, with Julius—just a couple of weeks before his wedding?

'Why me?' she asked carefully.

'I told you. Because you're a cook.'

Put that way, it sounded sensible enough. But her reactions weren't very sensible. Her heart began to feel as though it was beating at twice its normal pace.

'But can't you take them out to a hotel to wine and dine them?'

'I could,' he agreed. 'But that's defeating the object of it. I want to persuade them that our houses offer all the amenities and comfort and style that anyone would want in their home. The show house is already fully equipped. I want someone from the office who's both a secretary and a cook. You'll have to travel with me, work for me when I need you, and cook one very good meal——'

'I'm no good at Spanish dishes,' she cut in quickly.

'You don't have to be. It's the last thing we should offer Spanish clients on their home ground. Good international cuisine—French for preference.' He looked at her steadily. 'It won't be a holiday. I'll pay you extra, on top of what you get at the office. Will you come?'

'Can I think about it?'

'Fine. Provided you can give me an answer immediately after Christmas so that I've got time to sort out somebody else if you decide against it.'

He got up then, shooting out his wrist to check his watch in that familiar 'time is money' office manner. A wave of disappointment swept over her. Perhaps it was her fault he was leaving—he'd brought her Christmas presents, and an exciting prospect of earning more money, and all she'd done was insult him with a gratuitous reminder that he was engaged to Fiona. All because she couldn't cope with her own inappropriate desires.

'You wouldn't...like to stay for supper?' She wasn't sure it was a good idea to offer it, or that he would accept it even if he had the time to stay, but she meant it as a kind of apology for all the strange awkwardness of the evening which must surely be her fault.

He looked at her for so long that she thought she might have offended him further. Or was he trying to find a polite excuse that wouldn't hurt her feelings? Eventually he said, 'Amy, there's nothing I'd like better than to stay here with you and have supper but I don't think that's a good idea.' His tone was final.

'Why not?' she couldn't help asking.

He looked down at her as she got to her feet. Without her office high heels the top of her head reached his shoulder. 'Because just at the moment I can't afford to let myself be distracted by barbaric-looking ladies skilled in witchcraft.'

'You mean you've got work to do?'

He gave a wry smile. 'You could put it like that.'

She followed him into the hall and got his coat for him, watching him shrug it on, and then stood back when she opened the front door to let him pass her.

But when he was outside he appeared to hesitate, turning round to look at her, his expression again enigmatic. She remembered suddenly the description of him she'd first given Jess—'tallish, darkish, and definitely handsome...' That seemed tame now. He'd been like some high-powered electro-magnet as far as she was concerned from the very beginning, and she had no defences against the kind of physical power he had over her. Without even trying, he could fill her entire world for her if she let him.

Doing her best to ignore the jittery way her body was reacting to him, she was about to ask him if he'd forgotten something, when unexpectedly he caught her by the hand, and before she had a chance to react pulled her towards him until they were both standing under her spindly mistletoe.

She gave a little gasp as she fell against him, and glanced up at him, her lips parted, her slanting eyes wide with astonishment. He was smiling down at her. This time she could read a question in his eyes, and also a decision—he had already made up his mind what he was going to do. The question was for her; how was she going to react?

She couldn't even be sure herself—she could feel her heart beginning to race, while what could only have been a few seconds seemed to stretch out in an endless indecision. Feeling the way she did, she shouldn't even let him touch her... But she couldn't pull away. His hands were on her shoulders, and his fingers slid up round the back of her neck under her hair. 'Happy Christmas, Amy,' he said softly. Then her body seemed to make the decision for her, and everything changed—all the awkwardness between them melted away.

She didn't mean to slip her arms round him under his jacket, just as she didn't mean to raise her face so willingly for his kiss, but something seemed to take possession of her and she was prompted by pure instinct.

His mouth touched hers gently at first, and again she didn't mean to part her lips in such obvious invitation, but when he took her in his arms, pulling her against him and deepening the kiss, she forgot all about Fiona and any reasons she might have had for keeping aloof from him, and let herself kiss him back with all the generosity of which she was capable.

If she'd subconsciously tried to tell herself it was just a kiss under the mistletoe, and didn't therefore count in any serious way, that illusion was very quickly dispelled in the sudden heat that flared between them as his arms tightened round her. It was as though all the physical excitement that had been generated that first time at his flat, far from vanishing in the subsequent tensions and antagonisms, had been banked up—a fire storing its heat waiting to blaze into life again.

Just as before, all conscious thought left her, and she was aware only of her intense desire to please him as every inch of her body seemed to come alive in response to the increasing intensity of his kiss.

But, with a sudden sense of dismay, she was aware of the firm strength of his arms as he put her away from him. He was still gripping her shoulders, but holding her at a distance now. He was looking down at her, but he didn't say anything.

When she could find her voice she said shakily, 'We shouldn't have done that—what about Fiona?'

At his sharp indrawn breath, she could feel the renewed tension in him.

'I think Fiona deserves a dose of her own medicine just at present.' His tone was bitter. She couldn't read his expression. 'Fiona is my concern. Not yours.'

As though her heart had literally contracted at his words, she felt a sudden real pain then. She pulled back from him in pure reflex.

A dose of her own medicine—so that was what it was! She'd been misinterpreting the signals ever since he arrived. No wonder it had all been so awkward. Well, that certainly let her know her own position. He was only using her to get back at Fiona. What had just happened had nothing to do with her at all.

Tears suddenly pricking under her eyelids, she stepped blindly back into the doorway.

'Goodnight, Julius,' she said, as coldly as she could. 'Happy Christmas.'

And shut the door.

CHAPTER SEVEN

AMY didn't see Julius again until after Christmas, but the question of Spain preoccupied her almost to the exclusion of everything else. There was no real reason why she couldn't go. The extra money would be welcome, and Charlie and the cat could stay with Celia, which would solve the obvious home problems.

He'd asked her because she was a convenient combination of cook and secretary and for no other reason; and if she wanted proof that he had no real affection for her she had only to remind herself of that kiss under the mistletoe. She could feel very angry about that if she let herself. That had been about Fiona, some sort of revenge for whatever was going wrong with their relationship just then—not about Amy Thompson.

She was a little apprehensive about how the others would respond to her news when they eventually found out, but they were generous in their reactions.

'Four whole days with Julius!' Zoe sighed wistfully. 'You lucky thing!'

'Luxury hotels!' Jacquie enthused. 'I know because Julius has just asked me to make the reservations. Two nights in a five-star just outside Puerto Banus and another two in one of those wonderful *paradors* in Granada—yours is actually in the grounds of the Alhambra!'

That was more than Julius had told her, on his increasingly brief visits to the office after the Christmas break. Although she'd given him her decision to go to

Spain with him, his reaction had told her nothing of his feelings about it either way.

She was lying in her king-size double bed on her first night in Puerto Banus.

It had been all right back in England when they'd started off. Julius had, almost, teased her in the way he'd done when he'd visited her at home. She'd gone to work as usual on Tuesday morning—the day of their flight—bringing with her on the bus the one small suitcase she and Jess had packed the night before.

He had registered surprise at the sight of it.

'Is that *all* you've got?'

'But we're only going for four days, aren't we?' she had countered, a little dismayed.

'So what've you brought—four pairs of Charlie's rugger socks? You're the first woman I've ever taken away anywhere who didn't need an extra trailer for her wardrobe. Sure you haven't got another bag or three stashed away somewhere?'

That had introduced a few doubts—did he expect her to keep up with the jet-set executive image herself?

'I suppose Jess did tell me it was a bit unrealistic,' she offered. 'But I've never ever gone away with more than that. And anyway—I don't have any more suitable clothes.'

That shut him up very effectively, after he'd given her one very direct glance.

She saw the other two secretaries exchange looks of covert astonishment. They just couldn't wait for a gossip!

Julius drove to Heathrow only just in time for their flight. He was on the phone until almost the last minute, and then typically expected her to be ready to leave at two seconds' notice. By luck rather than good judgement, she was.

They were due to arrive in Malaga in the early evening, and he spent most of the three hours on the plane correcting sheets of reports, and studying legal documents. She sat next to him, conscious of the fact she was alone with him—the other hundred or so passengers didn't exist as far as she was concerned—and wishing he'd give her something to do. It was still office time, and she felt guilty about getting out a book to read. Eventually she found an old envelope in her handbag and began to write a shopping list for the dinner she'd have to cook. She and Jess had planned several alternatives to each course on the menu, just in case she couldn't get the ingredients she needed.

It didn't take long to jot down the main list, and she never for a moment forgot that Julius was sitting only inches from her. If she moved her knee only fractionally to the left, she could touch his. She found herself looking at his hands. He had strong, narrow hands with beautifully manicured nails, and where his shirt-cuff with its gold link was pushed up there was a dusting of fine dark hair on the back of his wrists. And as she stared at the pen moving with a fluid sureness over the paper she remembered the feel of those hands in her hair when he had kissed her outside her front door, and the way his fingers had caressed the back of her neck . . . and she remembered the time before that, at his flat . . .

The pen stopped. 'Want something to do?'

Suspecting sarcasm, she raised her eyes to his, and found him studying her. For one appalled moment she wondered if he had been able to see what she was thinking, and unaccustomed colour flooded into her face.

To her relief that amused him; he'd misinterpreted the blush.

'You don't have to feel guilty! There'll be plenty to get on with later this evening, and tomorrow. You'll have to eat on your own tonight—I'm seeing some clients as soon as we arrive. I'll take you into Marbella early tomorrow but I'll leave you to your own devices to do the shopping, and then I'll pick you up for lunch there before we go out to the development. You'll have all afternoon to prepare the dinner, and you can change at the villa.'

'Yes, *sir*!' She couldn't resist that, after the curt way he'd delivered her orders.

There was a twitch of a smile, and the business manner thawed briefly.

'Any more cheek from you, Miss Thompson, and I'll be leaving you on the runway at Malaga.'

But that 'Miss Thompson', although meant as a joke, put her firmly in her place. She thought about the implications of the fact that he wasn't asking her to have dinner with him that night; his reasons probably had nothing to do with consideration for her travel fatigue.

After a while she asked doubtfully, 'Are you sure you want me to join you for the business dinner tomorrow? I don't mind staying in the kitchen—in some ways it's a lot easier.'

'Miss the sight of you in your party socks? Not likely!'

He went back to his documents then, apparently switching into total concentration instantly.

Now, as she glanced round her room, she thought again that her words to Jacquie about a purely business trip might be far more accurate than she'd secretly been prepared for. Yes, they were in a luxury hotel all right. Her white-painted room, with its modern ceramic wall lights, mirrors, vast white wardrobes, its television set, its own well-stocked drinks cabinet, was almost fit for a film star. The hotel boasted smart little boutiques, and a heated outdoor pool, and only a few hundred yards away was one of the most fashionable beaches in Spain. She had her own balcony, which presumably had a view of the sea in daylight—but what was the point of it all when she wasn't going to get any time to enjoy it, and she had no one to share it with?

Julius must have arranged for the extra table to be brought into her room, on top of which stood an electronic typewriter—scarcely standard equipment for the average holiday guest! According to plan, he had disappeared almost immediately on arrival, and she had retired to her room to deal with the sheaf of papers he'd given her. Her only consolation was the fact that he wouldn't be hovering beside her, making her nervous, waiting for the finished typesheets.

She'd had a long, leisurely bath and resisted the temptation to take a long, leisurely gin with it—she didn't like the idea of Julius's most predictable expression once he was presented with the company bill to sign. He was absolutely certain to check every detail—'Miss Thompson, Room 302: four gins, four tonics—two per night of each—two half-bottles of champagne—one per night.' What else? Liqueurs after the supper she'd ordered up to her room perhaps? Grand Marnier? Cointreau? She gave a grim little smile. Serve him right for leaving her alone with a giant heap of typing to do while he went out to dinner! But she couldn't say he hadn't warned her.

It was after eleven when she finished typing. She wondered what he was doing. Was he still with his business associates, talking money and contracts in that quick decisive way of his, or had he already returned to the hotel? His room was one floor above hers. The hotel wasn't full. It seemed odd that people who were travelling together should be given rooms on different levels. Had he arranged that too?

For a while she sat in one of the comfortable armchairs and read the hotel magazines. There was an unexpected luxury in being able to wander round in her bedroom in the middle of winter clad in nothing but a fine silk nightdress. It was one her mother had given her as a birthday present. 'To fascinate your future husband with!' as she'd said with a twinkle in her eye.

Whether she'd been speaking in terms of the future when her daughter should already have a husband, or whether Amy was to wear the nightdress in order to catch the husband in the first place, she'd left deliberately ambiguous.

Now, as she lay in bed wondering how she was going to get to sleep, she thought of her mother. They had had a good relationship. Joanne Thompson had been an understanding and loving woman, and, with the first shock of her death over, Amy found that she was missing her more, not less, with every month that passed. Wearing the nightdress—which she seldom did; it was much too good to waste on Number 5 Estate Cottages— had brought back her mother's words as she had given it to her.

But oh, Mum, she said in her mind, what would you say if you knew it was somebody else's future husband I was in love with?

She *was* in love with Julius. She hadn't seen it quite like that before, but the discovery now was no surprise to her. Underneath, she must have known it all along.

Her mother and Julius would have liked each other. But it was only self-destructive to indulge in impossible dreams. And there wasn't much anyone could say to her present predicament—except, Give up your job. Don't spend any time with a man you can't have. The first of those was out of the question; and as for the second, well, there wasn't much she could do about that in the immediate future—she had three more days ahead of her, almost exclusively in his company.

Julius had told her to meet him for breakfast and she was nearly late. But she felt very satisfied with herself— she had typed everything he had given her. She knew she looked tired, and because she wore no make-up didn't do much to disguise it, but she looked smart, wearing her one respectable business suit with its fashionably short skirt—the one she'd worn for her interview—and she'd put her hair up.

She found Julius already seated at the table which he'd arranged they should share, and was uncomfortably conscious of the way he watched her as she approached.

She put the sheaf of typed papers with his notes down on the table and said before he could speak, 'I thought you might want these.'

He looked from her to the papers and back again. 'Did you get *any* sleep?' He sounded rather shocked— and disapproving. 'I didn't mean you had to do the lot of them last night!'

He made her feel as though she'd done something wrong again, and she was instantly on the defensive. 'Of course I slept. What time did you get in?'

'About midnight. So did you get time to do anything else last night?'

She tried not to sound defensive, and told him jokingly about fighting off temptation to empty the mini-bar.

He was looking at her strangely. 'Did you really think I'd be annoyed if you had a drink?'

She shrugged. 'It didn't seem very appropriate—after all, I'm here to work.'

'Yes, but not like a slave. Have whatever you like. I mean it, Amy. Anything—as long as I don't have to carry you paralytic out of a public bar.'

She gave him a sideways glance. He sounded serious about it, despite the final comment.

'You mean I've made you feel guilty because I worked last night?'

'Since you put it that way—yes. But I want you to enjoy this trip as well, and there's a lot lined up for today.

You can have tomorrow morning off when I go into Marbella again.'

He talked about plans for the development after that, and gave her a brief account of his business dinner the night before.

Then he drove her into Marbella, leaving her to explore on her own while he went to yet another business meeting. He gave her brief instructions as to how to get to the indoor markets, and told her to meet him at midday in the Orange Square.

'Where's that?' she asked, with a puzzled frown. What was this—an initiative test? She forgot for a moment that she was supposed to be Miss Efficiency.

'Know what oranges grow on?' he asked unhelpfully. It was his Zoe-and-the-dictionary tone. 'It's not far from here and named for obvious reasons. Sit at a table and then I'll look for you.'

And he was off after that, with a quick glance at his watch, striding away down the narrow street almost as though he couldn't get away from her fast enough. It reinforced the impression she'd got earlier—that he wanted to avoid her. His manner towards her most of the time was breezy and businesslike—not even quite the way he treated her in the office, but back at Prior's she was one of three secretaries and it shouldn't really matter how offhand he was. Now it did. It was a sort of personal statement about her.

She should never have come! Feeling the way she did about him, she'd had no right to agree to accompany him. She could have managed without the money, and he could have made other arrangements.

Shopping took longer than she'd thought; Jess's phrase book had limited uses. Julius was already waiting for her in the Orange Square when she eventually got back to it. He was right: the plaza was instantly identifiable by its deep green orange trees that lined the long rectangle. She caught sight of a familiar dark head as she made her way round the hedges that screened off the white-painted café tables and chairs in the centre. Her heart gave a little flip, as it always did when she saw him suddenly. He was sitting half turned away from her, reading a newspaper, his chair pushed back from one of the tables. There was something about him that would set him apart anywhere—and it wasn't only because he was the one man dressed in a smart business suit among the handful of more casually attired holidaymakers and residents who were enjoying the winter sunshine. She felt almost reluctant to meet him; it was increasingly painful to have him treat her in that dismissive way.

At that moment he looked up, with a quick glance round at the other tables, and then caught sight of her. Just for one fleeting second the look in his eyes was totally unexpected—almost as though he was really glad to see her. But then the look changed, and although she couldn't read the expression that replaced it she knew he was back to the efficient 'time is money' tycoon she was beginning to hate. She tried to match what she guessed would be his manner with a similar one of her own.

'Sorry I'm late. The phrase book wasn't up to things like ground almonds. Do you want to go straight to the development?'

He gave her a smile which didn't quite reach his eyes.

'I can see now why you used to bring so many carrier bags into the office—is that all for tonight?'

She was stacking an assortment of plastic carriers in one of the unoccupied chairs, very aware of the way he was watching her.

'All of it—but I didn't buy any wine. You didn't say anything about that.' She thought suddenly of the bottle he had given her for Christmas, and couldn't meet his eyes.

'No need. I've already arranged to have it delivered to the show house.' He might have told her! 'Did you have enough money?'

She nodded. He'd given her a stack of notes at breakfast.

He shot out a cuff then, and glanced at his watch. 'We'd better get a move on.'

'Is this a business lunch?' Would he be seeing yet more of his property dealers-bankers-lawyers and whoever else he was negotiating with? If he did, she'd be grateful to sink into the background purely as his secretary, one who wouldn't be expected to make any contributions in her own right. Perhaps there was something to be said for the way he was treating her after all.

'No. Just you and me. I thought you might need feeding up before tonight's effort.'

She was sitting opposite him now, and began to trace an invisible pattern with her finger on the surface of the table. 'Do you really want me to have dinner with you tonight or just to serve the meal?' She hoped he wouldn't think she was hinting that she wanted to join the party, but their last discussion on the subject had been inconclusive and she needed to know. It would make a difference to her arrangements.

'I want you to join us—like last time.' Last time with Chris and Maxine...when he'd kissed her afterwards and what had happened then had taken them way beyond their normal relationship.

A waiter appeared at Julius's elbow, but to her surprise he waved him away. She couldn't help feeling a little irritated at that—it had been a difficult morning and she would have liked a quick cup of coffee.

Julius stood up, with another glance at his watch. 'If we go now we'll just have time—the shops shut all afternoon.'

'Which shops?' she asked, puzzled. 'Time for what?'

He gave her a very direct look. 'To buy you a dress.'

Still sitting at the table, she stared at him blankly. 'What for?'

'I thought I'd get you something suitable to wear for tonight——'

'But I've got a dress!' She was sure she knew what he was implying: you look such a tatty mess most of the time I want to be certain you'll appear respectable in front of my business associates! Astonishment mingled with a sense of outrage, and she said indignantly, 'I've brought lots of clothes!'

He made no effort to hide his scepticism, a gleam of pure disbelief in his eyes. 'In one small suitcase?'

'I pack very economically!' she protested hotly. 'In fact, I've got not just one dress but two to choose from tonight!' Which was true—the second one had been a last-minute inclusion just in case real glamour was required. It might be a bit over the top for dinner, but maybe she'd wear it anyway. That'd show him!

'Amy, don't take this the wrong way——'

'Well, what way am I supposed to take it?' she demanded. 'Just because I wear the same things in the office every day doesn't mean I haven't got anything else!'

'You could accept it as a present.' There was a certain coolness now in his tone. 'I appreciate very much what you're doing for me on this trip and, if you feel you can't accept it on any other grounds, think of it as a bonus for a good secretary.'

She couldn't really believe her Miss Efficiency bid was *that* convincing. She gave him a direct look, her slanting eyes very blue with all the emotions she was trying to suppress. 'You don't honestly think I'm a good secretary!'

He held her gaze for a moment, then there was one of those unexpected flashes of amusement. 'Just at this minute I do. Make the most of it! Do you want a new dress or not? You've got about fifty seconds left to decide.'

There was no difficulty—she'd already made up her mind. Apart from her dislike of feeling patronised, she couldn't possibly accept something like that from him. It was the sort of present he should buy for Fiona, not her. But she felt abashed. His motives had probably been kind, and she'd just been very ungracious. 'No, thank you,' she said a little stiffly. 'It's very kind of you, but I'm afraid you'll just have to risk the fact that I might disgrace you.'

'I never thought you would for a moment,' he said quietly. 'You've got very exceptional looks.'

Her accusing stare masked a secret softening—he had paid her a real compliment! 'You told me more than once I had hair like red seaweed!'

'Would you believe some people like red seaweed?' His eyes were that enigmatic lucid grey, and their expression again baffled her. But she got the feeling suddenly that they should both tread very carefully, despite the attempt at a lighter tone.

He changed the subject immediately after that, detailing the rest of the afternoon, and filling her in briefly on the backgrounds of the three men she was to meet that evening as they found their way back to the car with all her purchases, before he took her to a restaurant for lunch. She would have enjoyed herself after that if there hadn't been that heightened sense of constraint between them again.

The development about which she had heard so much in the office turned out to be very impressive in reality. It was going to be a vast estate enclosed in its own park, offering a variety of homes, each one subtly different from the others. There was no sense of being on some holiday complex of identikit houses, as with others she had glimpsed along the stretch of coastline they had travelled. She could be genuinely enthusiastic about it, and was glad when Julius seemed pleased by her reaction.

The show house was a two-storey villa in its own garden, with a private pool. It was fully furnished as he had said and the kitchen was equipped like a cook's dream.

'There's even ice in the fridge,' she told him. 'Has someone been staying here?'

'I hired a woman to come in and check it out so that we'd have everything for tonight. She's coming back tomorrow morning to do the washing-up and clear up all the remains. It's up to her to dispose of any of the food we don't eat, so you can just leave all the stuff in here when we've finished dinner.'

'You don't want me to clear up?' She was surprised he was letting her off so lightly.

'You're acting as hostess,' he pointed out rather curtly. 'You can't be in here and entertaining the guests at the same time. Have you got everything you want?'

She wondered if he would offer to help her, the way he had done the time she'd cooked for him at his flat, but this time he was obviously expecting her to be the full professional and left her to it. She knew her disappointment was entirely unreasonable.

She found him sitting on the sofa in his shirt-sleeves when she went into the large living-room to set the table for the evening. He was working, a stack of papers on the floor in front of him and the phone on his knee. He glanced up at her and smiled, not the guarded smile he'd been giving her all day, but the genuine one he'd given her when he was with her and Charlie at home.

'All right?'

She smiled back. 'No problems.'

He glanced at his watch. 'I don't know how much time you need to get everything fixed for tonight, but

Spaniards eat late.' He'd already warned her that they wouldn't be arriving before nine. 'It could go on until the small hours of the morning. Go and have a rest. You'll need your energy for this evening.'

'But I'm not tired!'

'You will be.'

That sounded like an exit line—hers—and, disappointed by his tone, she turned on her heel and left the room. It was as though they were on a kind of emotional see-saw; she wondered if he was aware of his inconsistency, one moment treating her as though he cared about her as a person, and the next virtually dismissing her. Or was it that, because of the way *she* felt about *him*, she was over-interpreting what were really only very slight shifts in mood that had nothing to do with her?

She hadn't planned to sleep but there were four spacious bedrooms at her disposal; it seemed silly not to take advantage of one of them.

It was as though only seconds had passed when she woke with a start. Julius was calling her name and knocking loudly on her door. She wondered why he hadn't just come into the room. It wouldn't have been the first time he'd seen her in bed.

She had a bath after that, reflections of herself on all four walls amid the gold fittings and marble. Of the two possible outfits she had brought with her to wear on a formal occasion—a yellow jersey top and skirt in a flatteringly draped style, and a peacock-blue taffeta dress with a severely plain front but dramatically low-cut back—common sense told her that if she was unsure of the nature of the evening it would be safer to wear the yellow. But behind her arguments with herself that the sophistication of the other dress would give her confidence was the acknowledged desire to show herself, just once, to Julius in something that would make her look glamorous. So he thought she would turn up to dinner in the aesthetic equivalent of rugger socks and a Snoopy sweatshirt, did he? Well, she had something to show him!

She fixed her earrings, eyeing the tiny linked gold leaves critically in the mirror. They dangled in little chains each side of her slim neck and were very flattering, but she decided that any more jewellery might be overdoing it—she knew from the last time she had worn it that the peacock dyes of the taffeta were eye-catching enough. Instead she brushed her hair, sweeping it to one side over her shoulder, and as a concession to make-up darkened her eyelashes and touched a hint of blusher to her cheeks. Very satisfactory.

When she went back to the bedroom to put on the dress, she found that because she'd lost weight the shoulders had a tendency to slip down. The plunging V that exposed most of her back only made the problem worse, so she tried pulling the waist in tighter with a safety pin. It would keep the shoulders up, but the manoeuvre involved considerable contortions, and she couldn't see what she was doing. She decided to try the bathroom again—the arrangement of mirrors might give her some idea where to put the pin.

She didn't bother to close the door, angling herself so she could see a double reflection while she struggled with the pin. It was difficult to fasten it inside the fabric so that it wouldn't show. She pricked her finger twice in succession, swore, put it in her mouth—and then realised she had an audience. Julius was standing in the doorway, watching her.

She was aware from the way her pulses jumped that her heartbeat had suddenly quickened. Their eyes met in the mirror, her own wide and startled. She couldn't tell what he was thinking.

'Do you want any help with that?'

She took her finger out of her mouth, and shrugged, pretending to examine the tiny pink scratches the pin

had made, acutely aware of him. Then she bent her head
so that he couldn't directly see her expression while she
concentrated on the pin again.

'I can manage.'

Apart from anything else, it rather spoiled the effect
that he'd seen her dress before she was ready to show
herself to him, but she didn't want him to know that.
And if he thought she was overdressed—too bad. She
wouldn't take it off now.

He continued to watch her. She could sense it, even
though she didn't look at him in the mirror. She could
feel herself beginning to blush, her face growing hot.

For what seemed like a very long time neither of them
said anything. Then he was standing behind her, his
fingers touching hers as he took the pin from her. She
could feel his knuckles against her spine and every inch
of her skin seemed suddenly to have sparked alive as he
put his hand inside the waist of her dress. She tried,
unsuccessfully, to suppress a little shiver. He made no
comment. Instead he said, 'Tell me what you want to
do with this.'

Breathing quickly, she glanced up at him in the mirror,
but he was looking down at her back, the angles of his
cheekbone and jaw harsh in the artificial lights. She
thought he looked displeased. That made her all the more
nervous—and all the more determined not to change the
dress.

She explained briefly about the pin.

'Then bend forward and breathe in,' he instructed
curtly.

She couldn't even see in the mirror what he was
doing—she could only feel. His hand was against her
bare back. He must be fully aware of the fact that
underneath the dress she was half naked. Inside, her
bones felt as though they were melting and she had to
fight an overwhelming urge to turn round into his arms.

She couldn't help wondering how he'd react if she gave in to it. Both times he had kissed her before, the initiative had been his. But both times he had surely been prompted by his desire for revenge on Fiona. What would he do if she took the initiative now? He was standing very close to her; she would hardly have to move her own body to touch against the length of his.

She leaned against the basin, digging her nails into the palms of her hands, and stared down unseeing. She wished he'd say something, make the slightest move that would tell her that for a few moments she could give in to all the feelings she was finding it so hard to control. She could remember in a way that was almost physical how, those other times, a kiss that had started innocuously had turned into something very different, so that there had been no consciousness of anything or anyone else. She had given herself up to it completely, and she had known both times that he had done the same, whatever his original motives... Fiona.

She must be mad to let herself think like this.

'I suppose you do this for your fiancée,' she said, when she thought she might be ready to make it sound casual, as though it didn't matter to her. She didn't succeed. There was a thread of tension in her voice. She did—and she desperately didn't—want to defuse some of that intimate electricity that had begun to flow so dangerously between them from the moment he'd walked in.

'I have a sister,' he said, a little gruffly. 'And a niece.'

In other words, Fiona isn't the only woman in my life. But what was that supposed to mean? It was too risky to try to interpret, even though her body seemed to want to do that for her, a tiny charge of adrenalin firing something like hope through her veins. She felt as though she could hardly breathe at all now, and her heart seemed to be racing. She mustn't think of what the touch of his hands could do to her. She mustn't think about him in that way at all.

She tried to fix her mind on something else. The blue of her dress was an exotic dazzle before her eyes. What *did* he think of the way she looked? She met his eyes again in the mirror as his hands lingered at her waist.

She cleared her throat in a nervous manner. 'Go on— say it!' she challenged unevenly.

'Say what?' He sounded uncharacteristically wary.

'Tell me I'm overdressed.'

She caught the quick glance down at her back, before he looked at her again. 'Don't you think *under* would have been more appropriate?' There was a gleam in his eyes once more, but it wasn't humour this time and his voice sounded uneven, husky almost.

For five endless seconds everything seemed to hang in a balance, and the almost agonising longing that was sweeping over her threatened to engulf her completely.

Then as his hands went round her waist and he pulled her against him she felt the taut length of his body against her back. For a dizzying moment he looked directly into her eyes in the mirror and she read the desire in them clearly. Then she saw his dark head bent as his mouth touched the side of her neck, and she shut her eyes. A fiery weakness spread through every limb and with a little moan she let herself fall back against him, as he explored the sensitive areas of skin by her ear and along the line of her jaw with a concentration that both excited and scared her.

A new urgency quickly built itself inside her, until she turned impatiently in his arms, longing for him to take her lips. But even as she moved she felt his muscles tense, and she knew in the split-second before he released her that it was a rejection. Stepping away from her abruptly, he was at the door before she could fully realise what was happening.

His sudden exit broke the tension with such shattering abruptness that she almost collapsed. It was over so quickly, she couldn't believe for a moment he had left her—he hadn't even kissed her properly—and she had abandoned herself so completely in those few seconds. The tension having snapped, she could have screamed— or flung something to shatter all those acres of bright mirror round her.

It just wasn't *fair*! What was he trying to do to her? It was cruel to tease her deliberately—and if he didn't really want her, why couldn't he leave her alone?

There was more work to do in the kitchen before the guests arrived. Julius left her severely to her own devices, and she was both angry and grateful for the chance to regain whatever composure she could. That dangerous encounter in the bathroom had left her feeling very antagonistic towards him.

He came into the kitchen to find her after the Spaniards had appeared. She was already stripping off her apron, and he watched her while she whisked away the scarf she had used to tie her hair back, flicking a long swath of hair forward over one shoulder in a brisk and angry gesture. It was dark outside and she could see her reflection dimly in the kitchen window. His opening comment was ambiguous. 'They're never going to believe you're just my secretary!'

Just what was that supposed to mean? Her irritation with him grew. Surely they couldn't go on as though absolutely nothing had happened between them! Or maybe he thought they could? She looked up under her eyelashes, her slanting eyes suddenly flashing a very blue fire. 'Oh, but they will,' she said with acid sweetness. 'Just give me orders the way you did earlier today.'

He gave her a quick look at that, and then waited for her to leave the kitchen before him. She was burningly conscious of the way he now kept his physical distance from her.

It was just as well the dinner was everything she had planned it to be, and there were no unfortunate gaps or hitches between courses—she wasn't in the mood to deal with any culinary emergencies. Julius's business associates were older than him, with the exception of Miguel Diaz, a good-looking young Spaniard who very quickly made it clear that he, for one, had an unequivocal appreciation of her charms. The other two weren't indifferent to her either, but the only person she was really interested in was treating her with a cool detachment she found infuriating.

Underneath her easy social chat she was smouldering, her mind dwelling on the scene in the bathroom. Why had he initiated anything at all if he was only going to break it off like that? Did he think she'd been deliberately provoking him and he'd been intending to teach her a lesson? A strange sort of lesson if that was the case! Well, she'd teach him one now, and the message would be quite clear!

She flirted with Miguel openly at the table. She told herself it would scotch any suspicion that she was more to Julius than his employee, but her underlying motive was very different. She was choosing a method guaranteed to goad a further response from him if he genuinely did have any interest in her beyond a casual office friendship, and she also suspected she was playing with fire. But for this one night she just didn't care!

Miguel was certainly appreciative, making his admiration of her obvious, engaging her in conversation whenever he could, even following her into the kitchen to offer help with the coffee-tray.

'You are really Julius's secretary?' he asked.

She smiled, knowing very well what information he was after, and was surprised at how cool she managed to sound. 'Julius is getting married in a few weeks' time. It's only because he needs a cook that he's brought me with him. Yes, I really am his secretary—and that's all!'

She felt mean using Miguel like this. Through the open archway to the kitchen area she could see Julius talking to the other two Spaniards, but from the way he was glancing in her direction she knew he was watching her, and aware of her animated conversation with her new admirer.

'The coffee, Amy, please!'

The curt order was fired in her direction in the tone of an employer reminding her that she was neglecting her duty, and it riled her further.

It wasn't difficult to lead Miguel on to the subject of tourists and sights of interest in the surrounding area, knowing very well he would ask if he could take her out. They were satisfactorily launched into the topic as he carried the coffee-tray for her into the sitting-room and put it down on a low table.

'You have to work tomorrow?' Miguel asked, on cue.

Julius gave her a laser look. 'She's coming with me to Granada.'

He hadn't given her a chance to reply. She turned to him, a blaze of accusation in her eyes, but her voice was deliberately sweet. 'You said I could have the morning off.'

'Then that would be wonderful!' the unsuspecting Miguel exclaimed instantly. 'I have a lunch appointment I cannot break but before that—well, where would you like to go?'

And before Julius could intervene again she'd accepted the offer. She saw a flash of something very like real anger in his eyes.

It was decided that they would explore the surroundings of Puerto Banus, and maybe drive up into the hills if there was time. The discussion went on while she served the coffee and they were drinking the brandy and liqueurs that Julius had provided. All the time she was aware of Julius, deep in a conversation about property deals that couldn't include her. His manner was pleasant, even outwardly good-humoured, and there was nothing to tell anyone—except her—that there was anything wrong at all. He completely ignored her.

It was after one o'clock when the Spaniards left. Although it was late, she expected Julius to take some time to clear up the room, or at least to tell her to do it, but it was as though he couldn't wait to get out of the house. She was exhausted, but the unnecessary hurry over the departure annoyed her. She would have liked time to sort herself out.

'I told you I'd hired someone to deal with all this tomorrow,' he reminded her brusquely. 'There's no point your doing any of it. Get your stuff from upstairs and we'll go straight back to the hotel. Turn off the lights when you come down. I'm going out to the car.' And he was halfway through the front door before she'd had time to reply.

It didn't take long to collect her things from upstairs. She checked the kitchen before she left, and turned off all the lights as he'd instructed. He was waiting outside the front door with the car engine running when she got outside.

'What's the hurry?' she demanded as she got in beside him. 'I hardly had time to eat anything at dinner—there was lots of food left over in the kitchen and I'm starving!'

'Then order up something in the hotel.' His tone was curt. 'I've got a long day tomorrow. I don't want to hang about.'

She was silent after that. The earlier mood of recklessness had left her, but she still felt resentful and she could sense that he was angry. He had been in an unaccountable frame of mind all night... Maybe she hadn't really made him jealous at all—maybe purely as her employer he had disapproved of her behaviour with Miguel? But nobody else had seemed to mind—and they couldn't talk business *all* evening. So perhaps she had made him jealous after all? If so, she was beginning to regret it.

When they finally drew up outside the hotel, she couldn't bear the atmosphere between them any longer, and turned to him impulsively.

'Julius—just tell me what've I done that you don't like. Wasn't the dinner what you wanted?'

He looked at her sharply, as though he was surprised she should bring up the subject. In the inadequate light from the hotel entrance, his face was all angles and hollows, with cheekbones, straight nose and chin with its distinctive cleft accentuated. His eyes glittered. It wasn't so much his expression but his manner, and his voice, that gave away his reaction. 'The dinner was superb. Thank you. What makes you think I'm cross with you?'

'Because you've hardly said two words to me since the Spaniards left—you never even said it was all right! Is it because of the thing about my dress? After all that fuss about what I was going to wear I suppose you thought it was unsuitable! Or was it because I'm going out with Miguel tomorrow?'

He gave an impatient sigh. 'It's too late for all this now. I don't care who the hell you flirt with so long as it doesn't put them off a deal.'

He made it sound as though she'd been tiresome and childish in her demands for reassurance, and that made her stubborn.

'Then——?'

He turned to her suddenly, his eyes dangerous in the half-light.

'Leave it, Amy——'

'But——'

Then, without warning, his hands were on her shoulders, his fingers gripping into her flesh. 'You've been asking for this all evening!'

There was no doubting his anger now—she gave a little gasp as she tried to pull back, but his hold on her was much too powerful. His eyes stared directly down into hers, telling her something she couldn't read, then his mouth was on hers. There was no gentleness this time. It was as though he had set himself to plunder every inch of her, leaving her no defences. And she found herself wondering with what was left of her mind, How can he do this to me with only a kiss?

At last, he allowed her to pull away. She stared at him, her eyes wide with shock.

'Go to bed!' he said roughly. He suddenly seemed remote, hostile, completely apart.

Clutching her bag with all her things in it, she almost fell out of the car. She left the door open behind her, and stalked unsteadily into the hotel foyer.

She just got to her room in time. And then she started to cry. The evening had turned for no very clear reason into a complete disaster. Perhaps it was because she had played with fire—the very dangerous unpredictable fire that was Julius—and she was getting burned... Her childish attempt to provoke him now looked as though it was going to hurt no one in the end but herself.

She wished she'd never agreed to come to Spain. It was going to turn out to be the worst mistake of her life. She still had two more days to get through, and if tonight was anything to go by he was regretting his decision to bring her with him as much as she was.

CHAPTER EIGHT

THERE were gulls tossing on the wind against the massed clouds over the Mediterranean. Waves crashed and foamed over the wet sand, and Amy amused herself by dodging the water as she walked slowly back from Puerto Banus. There were no sunbathers now, no holiday umbrellas or foreign tourists, and although the cafés along the marina had been doing business the fashionable little harbour had a dead-season air about it. Some of the smart boutiques had been closed, and a couple of the restaurants boarded up.

Miguel had driven her up into the folds of the brown hills beyond the coast so that she could see some of the villages—the *pueblos blancos*, they were called, descriptive of the little whitewashed houses, visible for miles in that unwooded country. He had talked to her about Andalusia and local customs, and had been amusing and anxious to entertain her. She had done her best to respond to him, grateful to him for a morning that would otherwise have been spent alone. But, even though relations between them looked like a disaster, she wished it could have been with Julius.

They had stopped for coffee in Puerto Banus, and then, despite Miguel's eagerness to drive her back to her hotel before he left her for his lunch appointment in Marbella, she'd insisted on returning by herself along the beach. It might be her only chance to see it; she and Julius would be leaving for Granada after lunch.

It was nearly twelve o'clock when she started to make her way along the edge of the sea towards the hotel. If she walked slowly enough it might take her half an hour, and Julius could be back by one. He probably didn't want to see her, but that didn't stop her wanting to see him despite everything. They hadn't met at breakfast. She'd got up later than she'd intended, and found a note at Reception telling her he'd had to leave for his business appointment—but he could just have been avoiding her.

The wind whipped her long hair across her face. She stopped to take off her shoes, and then, checking quickly that there was no one about to see her, slipped off her tights so that she could walk at the very edge of the waves. She stuffed the tights in her jacket pocket and carried her shoes in one hand. She could make herself respectable again before Julius saw her.

Julius...

She told herself she must be in a very feeble mood— either that or she hadn't finished her crying from last night—but the tears kept pricking her eyelids as she walked, and she brushed one away impatiently. It had felt scalding-hot on her cold face. She was angry with herself for giving in to what she told herself was self-pity. So what if she loved a man she couldn't have? It happened to lots of people. Why should it be the end of the world just because Amy Thompson thought her heart was breaking? Anyway, he didn't love her, and she was being not only self-indulgent but *stupid* when she let herself think about him as anything to her but her employer.

He was angry with her about something, but she'd find out soon enough. He'd never been slow about letting her know in the past. But one thing it couldn't have been was the dinner itself—he'd said that was excellent—so that was all that mattered really. If her professional pride as a caterer was satisfied, that should be enough for her. Anything else she should apologise for and forget about, the way she did at the office. She wouldn't let herself think about what had happened outside the hotel when he'd brought her back. He'd said she'd asked for it. It was true—she had. She stopped to pick up a pebble, and flung it into the waves. Charlie could make them skip.

Icy foam spattered across her feet, ran a little further up the sand as the bubbles burst and then disappeared when the sea water withdrew. The end of her skirt flapped wetly against her legs, but she didn't care. It wasn't her 'office' skirt but one she wore at home, which she'd packed at the last minute. After all, she hadn't really wanted to impress Miguel despite that flirting last night. She felt rather ashamed of it now. Why don't I just cry? she thought. There's no one out here. Then when I've got it all out of my system I can be the ideal secretary for the two days we've got left, and I'll probably enjoy the trip a lot more. The perfect, common-sense solution.

She wasn't far from the hotel now. She glanced up from the water to check how much further she had to walk—and saw Julius standing on the beach just ahead of her.

Her heart suddenly turned over. Seeing him so unexpectedly like that, she knew that no common-sense reasoning in the world was going to talk her out of the way she felt about him. She loved him. Nothing was going to change that. She stood still, the cold water foaming over her feet, and looked at him.

He had his hands thrust into his trouser pockets, his feet apart, weight shifted slightly on to one leg. It didn't even strike her as odd that he should be there on the beach dressed in a suit intended for a boardroom. It was too far to see his expression, but he had been watching her.

He didn't move now, waiting for her.

Slowly she began to walk up towards him. He was on the firm sand, beyond the reach of the waves.

'Where have you been?' The demand was curt, and his eyes were coldly angry. It was the first time she'd ever seen him quite like that.

'You—you said I could have the morning off!' She was taken aback by the hostility of his reception.

He gestured at the wide expanse of beach. 'You could at least have told me where you were going. I might have needed you.'

'But you did know—Miguel took me out for a drive!' Her voice rose in protest. 'We were discussing it last night, after dinner. And anyway, you said you wouldn't be free till one.'

'The meeting finished early.'

She didn't quite know what to reply. Why should he be so angry again all of a sudden? She hadn't done anything wrong.

They stood, glaring at each other, the wind whipping long streamers of red hair round her face. She pushed it back off her forehead, and held it, to keep it out of her eyes. It was lifting his hair too, in an uneven ridge of dark little feathers.

'Where's Miguel?'

She shrugged. 'He had to go to a business lunch. He wanted to bring me back to the hotel, but I preferred to walk.'

She wished he'd stop looking at her like that.

'Where did he take you?'

'For a drive in the hills. Around. Does it matter?'

'Is he seeing you again?'

She laughed awkwardly, without humour. 'No, of course not! How could he, even if he wanted to? We're going to Granada this afternoon.'

She couldn't read the look he gave her—the light in his eyes was less aggressive; more as though he wanted to read every single thought. His laser look—with an indefinable difference.

'What exactly have I done wrong?' she asked defensively. 'Shouldn't I have accepted an invitation from someone you're doing business with, is that it? I'm sorry. I didn't know.' She knew she didn't sound in the least apologetic, just antagonistic, driven to defend herself by the need to hide her real feelings.

He drew a visibly deep breath, and took his hands out of his pockets. 'No. You haven't done anything wrong.'

She stood her ground. 'Then was it the meeting? Didn't it go well?'

'Forget it. I'm sorry.' He took a step closer, then looked at her narrowly. 'What's the matter?'

'Nothing.'

'You've been crying. What is it?'

'I haven't. It's the sea wind—it stings my eyes.'

She could tell by his expression that he didn't believe her. Without a word he took the shoes from her, and to her astonishment touched her hand, lacing his fingers through hers and pulling her towards him. As always, her body reacted at the contact, but she deliberately kept her mind from all speculation. If he could kiss her the way he had last night, holding her hand meant nothing to him.

'Come on,' he said. 'Let's go back to the hotel and get a drink.'

They walked slowly, in silence for a while, Julius matching his stride to hers. His clasp was firm and warm; despite her surprise at the gesture, she was glad when he didn't let go of her hand. She decided it was an apology for the way he'd just spoken to her, even though he didn't seem willing to explain to her what had provoked it.

After a while he said, 'It wasn't until I overheard you talking to Miguel last night that I realised in how many ways your father's death must have changed your life. Do you still miss your parents very much?'

His guess as to why she'd been crying? If that was what he thought, it was better he should go on thinking it. But she hadn't known he'd been paying so much attention to her conversation with Miguel—it had only been a passing reference.

'Yes,' she said quietly. 'And I'm only just beginning to find out what they meant to me.'

He was silent again, and then went on, 'I also realised you must have had a very different sort of life with them. I hope you didn't——' He broke off, and then started again, 'You obviously thought I insulted you when I offered to buy you a dress yesterday. It was only meant as a . . . token of appreciation for your coming on the trip with me.' She had never heard him sound so careful in his choice of words with her. 'Was that why you wore what you did last night?'

She gave a rueful smile. 'Then you did think it was a bit over the top?'

'No. I didn't think anything of the kind.'

Now that he seemed more approachable, she couldn't resist skating perilously near that thin ice. 'It seemed to have quite effect on Miguel.'

He looked down at her. 'He wasn't the only one.'

Her heart gave that little leap suddenly, but then the light in her eyes died just as quickly. Making him jealous had been something she'd promised herself she wouldn't try to do. Now instinct warned her not to gratify her curiosity any further. The consequences could be more disastrous even than last night. She wasn't prepared for him in this mood, and it would be both humiliating and unwise to have to acknowledge her own feelings to him.

'Amy——' He stopped walking, pulling her back to face him and in those few seconds her mind was working desperately. She didn't want an explanation—she didn't even want him to say anything that would alter the awkward atmosphere between them, which seemed infinitely preferable now to any sort of discussion.

'About last night. I didn't mean to upset you.'

'You didn't,' she lied.

'I think I did,' he said gently. 'But it was nothing to do with the dinner——'

'It's all right,' she interrupted quickly. 'You don't need to explain.' She detached her hand from his. They had stopped by the boarded path that ran from the hotel down to the beach over the softer sand that was hard to walk on—they were almost at the hotel.

'I have to go back to my room to change before lunch,' she said, without looking at him. 'Can I have my shoes, please?'

He handed them to her, his eyes still on her as though he was trying to read that careful expression that shuttered her face.

'Amy, I have to talk to you——'

She was already walking ahead of him. 'It's OK,' she said with false lightness. 'I've told you, you don't have to explain anything.'

'Amy——!'

But she was almost running as she reached the hotel foyer, still in her bare feet. She didn't look back.

During the drive to Granada that afternoon they were carefully polite to each other, and to her intense relief he showed no inclination to open up the topic she was now so wary of, seeming preoccupied and remote. It was dark when they arrived. She had slept for the last part of the route, but although he woke her when they reached the outskirts of the city she only had a very sketchy impression of the historic provincial capital—just street-lights and rows of dark trees as they drove up the hill to their *parador*. She remembered Jacquie telling her that it was in the gardens of the Alhambra.

The *parador* was unlike any hotel she'd ever stayed in, the entrance hall that of an old mansion with its azulejos—coloured Andalusian tiles—and old Spanish furniture. There were paintings hung on the walls and antique ornaments, and through carved wooden doors she glimpsed an enclosed courtyard.

She was relieved that Julius would be leaving the hotel almost immediately for his business appointment. If it hadn't been for indulging in that silly whim the evening before, she could have been enjoying the prospect of the hours they would spend together the following day, but now she felt as though they were on a knife-edge. The slightest impulse could split their precarious relationship apart. She sensed that she could only avoid that happening if she preserved the situation exactly as it was, no matter how artificially.

But her plans for passing an uneventful evening alone were dramatically altered by the unexpected arrival of Miguel—and, unable to resist his dazzling smile and very persuasive charm, she agreed to go out to dinner with him. It was flattering to have been chased all the way from Marbella. It also kept her from brooding on the situation with Julius.

She enjoyed the evening, but after a while the compliments and rather too obviously loaded remarks began to get on her nerves; she didn't want the evening to have to end with an argument, and took a very public and brisk leave of him when they finally returned, late, to the *parador*.

It was as she reached the staircase that, glancing back, she was aware of Julius entering the hotel. He didn't see her, his eyes going straight to Miguel. She took the stairs two at a time in her haste to disappear from view, but she had the feeling that he had caught sight of her.

She was right. And breakfast the next morning was very nearly a further disaster: they were almost instantly into a replay of the conversation on the beach. His mood seemed to have changed since all that edgy politeness of the previous afternoon, and it didn't take her long to account for the hostility.

'Enjoy your dinner last night?' It was like the opening of an attack.

'Yes, thank you.'

A pause. 'What was Miguel Diaz doing here?'

She kept her eyes on her coffee-cup. Surely they couldn't be about to launch into the discussion she was so afraid of right in the middle of the dining-room?

'He came to see me—why?'

'Did you ask him to?'

'Of course I didn't!' She glanced up then, to find him watching her, his expression unusually grim. A muscle twitched at the corner of his mouth. She went on as casually as she could, 'He knew I was coming here— and I'd told him you were going to another business meeting tonight. He didn't have anything else to do so he thought he'd come along and take me out to dinner. Anyway——' she tried to sound as though she had no idea of the answer he was going to give '—how did you know?'

'He was here when I got back last night. You were on your way upstairs. Is that all he did—take you out to dinner? You don't look as though you've had much sleep.'

A waiter, who couldn't have chosen a worse moment if he'd tried, was suddenly at her elbow with a basket of elaborately arranged flowers.

'Señorita Thompson? These are for you.'

She didn't need to find the card, buried in the profusion of pink and blue ribbon that decorated the side of the basket, to know they were from Miguel. And, judging by the look on his face, Julius was in no doubt about who'd sent them either—his expression was thunderous. They seemed to lend substance to the veiled accusation in his last remark—that she had spent the night with Miguel.

His final remark had been a deliberate insult, but it wasn't that that hurt her. Last night, lying awake, she had given a great deal of thought to Julius's recent treatment of her, and had come to some painful conclusions. She would avoid an explanation between them for as long as she could, but she was sure he was jealous of Miguel, and that must mean he wanted her himself. It couldn't be love—not when he was so deeply involved with Fiona—and that was where she found herself caught in an impossible situation. If it wasn't love, she didn't want it. But if it *was* love, she could never live with the knowledge that she had bought her own happiness at the expense of another woman's.

Now the inquisition over Miguel only served to confirm her suspicions. Abruptly, she pushed her chair back, but Julius must have guessed her intention and before she could get away from the table his hand shot out and his fingers clamped themselves round her wrist.

'Sit down, Amy!' It was an order, not a polite request, and she resented it at once. His eyes were steely. 'I've got to talk to you. There's something I must know.'

She hesitated, looking down at his hand, but he didn't slacken his grasp. Reluctantly she sat down again. There wasn't much else to do in the circumstances. She couldn't really think straight; all she was aware of was the pounding beat of her own heart, so loud he must be able to hear it too.

'Does it have to be now, this minute?' she asked in a strained voice.

He released her wrist. 'No. Finish your breakfast. Then we'll go out for a walk.'

But she couldn't eat. She was aware all the time of his impatience as he drained his coffee-cup and then flicked over the pages of a Spanish newspaper, his thoughts clearly distracted, waiting for her. She felt almost sick with nerves. They had reached the crisis she had been trying to avoid.

They left the *parador* to enter the ancient gardens. The approach under the street-lamps the night before hadn't prepared her for the size, or the splendour, of the buildings that lay around her. The winter morning sunlight warmed the many walls and turrets to the colour of pale honey, and the very air seemed to sparkle. Almost forgetting for a moment the reason they were there, she turned impulsively to Julius, and found him studying her face rather than the scene before him.

'Like it?' he asked.

She gave a tense smile, and looked away again. 'Of course!'

Unexpectedly, he took her hand, and they walked up to the entrance to the palace area together—a peace gesture perhaps? The way he was touching her didn't have to mean anything, except that she couldn't be in-different to it. From that moment the atmosphere between them seemed subtly to change. Some of the antagonism vanished, though the tension remained; she felt as though they were walking on glass.

They crossed sunlit courtyards, admiring the arches carved with fretwork like cream lace, the old wall tiles, the stone basins splashing with mountain water. It felt unreal to her, as though she were watching it all in a film, her true self elsewhere, the crisis looming closer with every minute that passed. Julius put his arm round her shoulders as they stood to examine the twelve stone lions that surrounded one of the fountains, and again she was conscious of him watching her, rather than the scene before her.

'You're very quiet,' he said at last.

She only had to relax a little to lean against him. Don't do this; don't indulge in something that will only make you unhappy afterwards, a voice kept repeating in her head. But she let herself touch him, the length of her thigh against his, her arm against his side.

'It's so beautiful—I can't find words for it.'

Suddenly, her mood unstable as it had been since she got up that morning, she was flooded with a poignant, bittersweet happiness all the more intense because she knew it wouldn't last. She knew all the consequences, and she didn't care. She would pay later.

He made no comment, and they walked on; but he didn't take his arm away. She was conscious of the weight of it across her shoulders as they left the walled areas of the palaces and fortress. All the time she was wondering when he would introduce the topic she so desperately wanted to avoid.

The long avenues of tall dark trees led to the famous gardens of the Generalife. Massive sheltering hedges towered over them like walls, screening formal gardens of stunted little winter roses, yet more fountains and perfect orange trees, their dark leaves jewelled with fruit. She was only half aware of them—the inevitable moment ticked closer with every second.

Julius found a tiny orange—not much bigger than a large nut, its leaf still attached. He gave it to her.

'A souvenir.'

She smiled tensely, examining it. 'You're not supposed to pick these.'

'I didn't. Fate put it in my path.'

She met his eyes this time. His words held more than their obvious meaning, and his eyes told her a message she didn't want to read. She looked away quickly, and put the orange in the pocket of her jacket.

They sat down by the wall, looking across the valley. The trees were leafless, but the air crisp and clear like a summer wine, the quintessence of sunlight. There was a splashing of water running continually through the fountains and sluices. Even the noise of traffic from the city was too far away to encroach on the magic, and for a while they were entirely alone.

She closed her eyes, relaxing a little for the first time. 'This is almost like Eden,' she said unguardedly. 'A dream I don't ever want to wake up from.'

She knew instantly from the quality of his silence that, after all her caution, she was the one now who had opened that dangerous gate to the discussion she had been trying to avoid. She knew too that he was looking

at her, even though there was nothing but an orange-
red blur of light against her eyelids.

'Man, woman and garden.'

Her reply was deliberately double-edged. 'There's even
forbidden fruit.'

'Not forbidden,' he said slowly. His voice was very
tense. 'Only unwise.'

She opened her eyes then, and looked at him, struck
by his tone. 'I meant the little oranges in the courtyard
of the fountains,' she said carefully.

'Did you?'

His gaze held hers, and she could feel a thousand tiny
pulses beginning to flutter all over her body, while her
heart beat painfully against her ribs. She was on the very,
very edge... something she so desperately wanted, and
couldn't let happen.

Her arm was resting along the back of the bench. He
was sitting at a little distance from her. He took her hand,
turning it over, studying the palm, and it took all her
self-control not to lean forward so that he would take
her in his arms.

'Do you believe in fate, Amy?'

The question took her by surprise. She tried to sound
flippant, and then regretted her reply—it seemed all
wrong for the place, and the time, but she didn't dare
give any other. 'Are you asking me to answer that as a
witch?'

He looked at her hand, lying passively in his own, and
slowly turned her palm to his, linking his fingers through
hers. His expression was serious, his eyes still studying
their joined hands. 'I'm not asking you to foretell our
futures. Until recently, I'd have said there was no such
thing as fate intervening in someone's life—your future
was very much what you made it. And I was doing my
best to make mine according to what I thought was a
pretty sensible plan.'

'And then?'

He looked at her directly, his eyes an intense grey. 'And then something—maybe fate—came along and the plan wouldn't work any more.'

His fingers unexpectedly tightened on hers, and he stretched out his other hand to caress the side of her face. His touch affected the whole of her body and involuntarily she found herself leaning towards him, drawn by that force now too powerful for her to resist. Then, without being quite aware of how it happened, they were both standing pressed desperately close, and his arms were round her, locking her from the escape she had no intention of seeking. He had kissed her three times before, but it had been nothing like this slow, controlled persuasion that ravished every sense, until without thought she gave herself to it utterly. She was conscious of every contour of that hard, muscled frame against her own, and she was both shocked and elated to realise how much he desired her.

When finally they broke apart, she was shaking. She took a step towards the wall and leaned against it, staring out unseeing over the valley.

Julius moved to stand beside her, close, but not touching. 'Do you know why I brought you here with me—to Spain?'

She tried unsuccessfully to control her voice. 'You told me you needed me as a cook—and a secretary.'

His reply sounded impatient. 'Cook, secretary, yes—but I didn't have to bring either. There were other ways of arranging it.' He went on without waiting for her to comment. 'I wanted to be able to get to know you away from the office, and away from home, where I couldn't see you as often as I'd have liked. I suppose——' He paused, as though to find the words. 'I suppose I wanted to make certain of something I knew already...'

She felt his hand on her shoulder, and he drew her round inexorably to face him, forcing her to meet his eyes. 'I love you, Amy. I think I've loved you since that first afternoon you walked into my office. I love you and I want you.'

It was what she secretly longed to hear, and what she was afraid of. She did her best to sound cold, avoiding his gaze. 'Just because we don't seem to be able to control our physical reactions when we get too close, it doesn't mean to say we love each other! You can't change your life because of something like that—and you can't do this to Fiona. It isn't fair. You don't really love me— there's no such thing as love at first sight. We're just physically attracted to each other...'

His answering sarcasm made her flinch. 'Do you honestly think I'm such a prey to my lusts I can't cope with a few days in the company of a pretty secretary?' He touched the side of her jaw, with hard fingers, turning her face towards him. 'No, Amy, it's not that and you know it. I care about you. I want to make you happy— and I want the right to be with you. Always.'

'But Fiona——'

He interrupted her impatiently. 'Do you really think I'd be doing this without a thought for Fiona? You must have a very low opinion of me!'

'It's not that——'

'It *is* that, Amy! Would it really be fair to her to marry her when I love someone else?'

She turned away abruptly to hide the tears in her eyes. Despite his angry impatience, the words had an unmistakable sincerity.

'Even before I met you there were problems with our relationship. We're not really suited to each other; we never were.'

'Then why did you get engaged to her, or she to you if you weren't suited?' she demanded desperately.

There was a long silence. Then he said, 'I can't go into all the reasons—you'll just have to trust me—but the situation wasn't simple when I met Fiona. It seemed to both of us that we had a good enough basis for marriage. She had reasons to be wary of passionate involvements, and I—well, at that time I didn't think that kind of passion was a very useful guide when it came to choosing a wife. Apart from that, we got on very well socially, and we liked—continue to like each other very much.' It wasn't a very satisfactory answer, but his tone warned her not to probe any further.

'But even if you've changed your mind now,' she protested, 'it doesn't mean that she has!'

'Amy, did you take in anything I said?' He sounded exasperated.

She ignored him. 'You're only two weeks away from marrying her!'

He took a deep breath. 'My marrying Fiona in two weeks' time isn't going to ensure her happiness either now or in the future, and if it's any consolation to you I suspect that she has seen that for herself!' He paused for a second, as though to check himself. And then said more quietly, 'It's something I'll have to sort out when I get home——'

She stared at her fingers, twisting them tightly together as she rested her hands on the top of the wall. She just had to see this through to the end. She had never imagined it could be so difficult.

'If you do this Julius, you must do it because it's the right thing for both of you—not just because you want me instead of her!'

She tried to pull back from him as he put his arms round her, drawing her against him despite her resistance. She held herself stiffly, determined to ignore what the contact was doing to her. To break off his engagement to Fiona because he genuinely believed that they were not suited to each other was very different from breaking off from one woman in order to have another. If he thought Amy herself was ready to fall into his arms, she would never know which was the true reason. There was, she realised, only one sure way to find out.

She had to give him up, utterly. And then wait to see if his marriage plans to Fiona were resumed.

As she felt him draw back from her a little, she glanced up to find him staring down at her.

'Amy, I have to know,' he said carefully. 'I have to hear you say it—do you love me?'

There was a long pause while she looked at him, praying for the composure that would let her convince him. She knew she was going to hurt him.

'No. I don't love you,' she lied.

It was the hardest thing she had ever done.

His eyes searched hers, at first in blank disbelief. Then his expression changed. His look became shuttered, his face set, his mouth a grim line.

They stood facing each other, saying nothing. She had no idea how long they remained like that. It was as though some sort of storm had swept right through her, leaving her empty. She couldn't even guess at what Julius might be feeling.

CHAPTER NINE

IT WASN'T going to last much longer. Surely she could put up with just a couple more weeks for the sake of the money?

Of all the catering jobs she'd ever done, this had to be the least suited to her particular talents—and the most exhausting. But she hadn't left herself much choice. Walking out of Prior Harding's like that meant she'd had to take the first job she could find. Acting as cook-cum-housekeeper at a girl's boarding-school definitely wasn't her ideal role in life, she thought wearily. Thank goodness she was only an emergency stopgap, and Mrs Rogers, whose place she was taking, would be back soon. There had been unexpected illness in her family, and because the school had had to find a replacement at such short notice the money was very good. In theory, it was a full month's employment, which would allow time to look around for something else. In practice, it didn't seem to be working like that.

Getting up before six to prepare breakfast with two part-time helpers, from the moment she got into those kitchens—very much in need of modernisation—she never seemed to have a second to herself for the rest of the day. No sooner had she finished breakfast than she had to start on lunch. It wasn't that she didn't have any time off, it was just that she had to use it to keep up with herself. By half-past eight in the evening she was completely worn out.

Apart from the money, the only advantage to the job was that it gave her very little time to brood over what had happened in Spain, and the end of her relationship with Julius. His image hovered in the background of everything she did, but it was really only in bed at night that she had time to think about him.

They had left Granada early on that last morniug. He had been unusually thoughtful, and instead of that curt businesslike tone that had characterised his manner on much of their trip he had been gentle with her in a way that made it all so much harder to bear. She had found afterwards the little orange he had given her in her pocket, and thought of their conversation. 'Forbidden fruit,' she had called it. 'Not forbidden,' he had said. 'Only unwise...' In the circumstances, it had been unwise even to talk about what was happening between them. It would have been better if they could have left the whole thing unexpressed, then she wouldn't have had to lie to him, and he could have broken off his engagement to Fiona without the decision involving her. She was aware that in her position other women might not have seen her difficulty, but she could only be true to what she felt to be right. She had to be true to herself.

Julius hadn't appeared in the office on Monday, and the others had been avid for gossip of the trip. She'd given them endless details of the hotels, the food, the places they'd visited, Julius's Spanish contacts—all, as far as she was concerned, utterly meaningless now—until Zoe had demanded, 'But what about Julius? What was it like to spend all that time with him?'

She'd pulled a little face. 'Just the same as at the office.' It hadn't contented them, but it was all she had been prepared to say. She *wouldn't* talk about him.

When Dennis had told them that Julius had had to go on another business trip and wouldn't be in for the rest of the week, Jacquie had looked at her significantly. 'Gone to see Fiona. It's less than two weeks until the wedding.'

Amy had had to turn away quickly to hide what she knew would give away far more of what had gone on in Spain than she would ever tell anyone—even Jess.

She hadn't let Dennis know until the Friday of that week that she wouldn't be coming back. She'd felt terrible about it, but it wasn't until that morning that she'd got the offer of another job, and she'd been afraid that the news of her intention might get through to Julius too soon—before she could avoid a confrontation between them.

'It's—it's home problems,' she said unsteadily. 'I have a young brother—things are very difficult at the moment.' Dennis could see that she was upset, and hadn't prolonged the explanations, despite his obvious dismay. He'd offered to get in a temp if she needed a couple of weeks to sort things out. She had been consumed with guilt. He had been trying to make it as easy for her as possible to resume her job once the mythical 'home problems' had sorted themselves out, and what she had really been doing was walking out on him.

She couldn't bring herself to say goodbye to the others—unlike her employer, they would be sure to demand more satisfactory explanations, and their concern, which she wouldn't deserve, would be more than she could bear. She had had to get away before Julius came back—and before he had time to do anything about it.

It was Jess who had shown her the advert for the cook-housekeeper when she had first told her of her intention to leave Prior's. Guessing that there must be a lot more behind the brief story of 'not getting on with Julius' that Amy had told her with some reluctance after her return from Spain, Jess had wisely held her tongue. But she'd offered to solve the problems of Charlie and the cat by the simple solution of moving into Number 5 Estate Cottages herself.

'I'll look after everything and make sure there isn't a freeze-up if the weather gets cold. It's only four weeks, for heaven's sake. Just promise me you'll ring every evening to talk to Rasputin. I hate to think of you all by yourself down there in the wilds of the West Country.'

Amy had given a humourless grin. 'With two hundred schoolgirls to cater for, I'm not going to get much time to be alone, am I?' she'd pointed out.

Although she hadn't seen much of the girls themselves, at least half her forecast had proved accurate. She was constantly in the company of the kitchen staff, and even shared her tiny flat with one of the matrons. But she did ring Jess every night, feeling a sort of outcast in her self-imposed exile.

There was no chance of hearing anything from Julius. Both Jess and Charlie had been sworn to secrecy as to her whereabouts. He had to believe she'd gone out of his life for good, although, the way their last conversation had ended, it looked more as though he was the one who had gone out of hers. So it was no use indulging in fantasies in which he rode up on a white horse to tell her they could be happy together forever, and snatched her away from a life of drudgery; he didn't even know her address.

You're turning into a weed, Amy Thompson, she'd told herself sharply. But it didn't have much effect.

She'd spoken to him just once since they'd come back from Spain, on the phone, on the Monday morning she'd left to take up her job at the school. He must have heard of her decision only minutes before by the sound of it.

'What the hell is this Dennis has just been telling me— you're not coming back?' He sounded very angry. She didn't answer. Her heart was pounding so violently that she felt sick.

'Come on, Amy, what's this new problem with Charlie?' he demanded impatiently. 'It can't be so bad a couple of weeks off, if that's what you want, won't solve it!'

'I don't want a couple of weeks off,' she said, so low that she wondered if he'd hear her. 'I've left.' It was awful, just hearing his voice again.

'Don't be silly. You can't afford to—what are you going to do for money?' A note of concern softened the anger just a little that time.

'I've got another job.'

It was as though she'd just chucked a grenade into the conversation. The silence was explosive. If the receiver had burst into flames in her hand she wouldn't have been surprised. Then he said, in a voice of tight control which was somehow worse than if he'd shouted at her, 'You've got a perfectly good job here. Why walk out on Dennis when he needs a full-time secretary who knows the ropes?'

'I'm not just walking out on him!' she argued with guilty desperation. 'We discussed it—he understands! I'm sorry...I didn't want it to cause any trouble. You don't...you don't have to pay me——'

'For heaven's sake, Amy! This has got nothing to do with the money.' There was a pause. Then, 'Is it by any chance because of what happened in Granada?'

She couldn't answer.

'Right,' he said then, coldly. 'Enjoy your new job, Amy.'

And the line went dead.

She stared at the phone in a sort of shocked helplessness. It was somehow so final. She'd never meant it to happen like that, and never in her life had she felt so desolate.

In her mind ever since she'd been ticking off the dates on a secret calendar, each nearer to the day of Julius's wedding, until last night when she hadn't slept at all.

She was in an agony of suspense—she had to find out, had he or hadn't he married Fiona? If he had, she would have to try to forget him. If he hadn't—but surely if they'd cancelled the wedding then everybody must have known for days? Why hadn't she thought of that before? She could have found out if she'd had the nerve to ring Jacquie at the office. Surely all the guests would have been told as soon as possible, and Jacquie, of all people, would have known about it?

She couldn't bring herself to ring Prior's, but she thought Jess might have heard something. She had. The wedding hadn't taken place.

'How did you find out?' she demanded, as soon as she could trust herself to say something.

'Julius has been round here. I'd have told you before, only you said you didn't want to hear about him. He came to take Charlie out last Sunday.'

'What about Fiona? Did he say anything about her?'

Jess's reply was vague. 'He didn't really talk about her. Listen, are you still determined not to tell him where you are?'

Amy was adamant. She didn't want to nourish any false hopes, and anyway, it would be impossible to find a time or place in her present circumstances for the kind of interview she and Julius might have.

'Oh, well.' Jess sounded resigned. 'You've only got another couple of weeks and a bit. Let me know when you've decided which trains you're catching, and Mum'll meet you at the station if I can't. We'll celebrate your escape from that place—it sounds awful!'

Two weeks and a bit. It felt like a lifetime.

She tried not to think about Julius on the train journey back to Oxford, but, however far away from him she started off, her thoughts inevitably led back to him. He hadn't married Fiona. Well, he had told her he wasn't going to. Perhaps she shouldn't have run off like that. Perhaps she should have waited quietly to find out what would happen. She should have trusted Julius more. She had made a lot of assumptions about the situation and acted on those, and although she hadn't thought so at the time she had behaved very impulsively on her return from Spain. She still felt bad about leaving Dennis and the others the way she had.

She tried to think about Charlie, and Jess, and fix her thoughts on seeing Celia at the station. It would be like a holiday coming home again after the way she'd been working, even if she did have to go out immediately on another job hunt.

There was no sign of Celia when the train drew into Oxford, but she could have been waiting on the opposite platform, by the station entrance. Amy gathered up her bags, slinging one over her shoulder and carrying the larger of the two. It was just as well she hadn't taken much luggage with her.

She kept to the back of the crowd of commuters, hoping to spot Celia among the passengers waiting for the next train, but when the crowd began to thin there was still no sign of her. She couldn't have forgotten the day, could she? Another unlucky mnemonic?

She'd just decided to explore the bookstall to help pass the time when someone she thought she recognised came through the entrance hall, glancing around as she went. It was unmistakably Fiona Harper-Maxwell—she recognised the blonde hair and the confident walk. She looked worried.

A strange feeling went through Amy at the sight of the girl Julius had been going to marry. It was a mixture of familiarity—she suddenly brought Julius himself very close—and wariness. Then Fiona caught sight of her, and instantly came towards her.

'Amy—you *are* Amy, aren't you?'

Amy was taken aback. 'Yes, but——' Why should Fiona be looking for her? She seemed surprisingly friendly.

'I'm awfully late—I'm sorry. You were expecting a friend called Celia?'

'Has anything happened?'

Fiona gave her a reassuring smile. 'No, no. Everything's fine. I don't know if you remember me, but I'm Fiona—we met briefly one night at Julius's house when you came to cook?' She didn't pause for a reply. 'I've been instructed to fetch you—I'll explain why as we drive. Look, do you mind if we go now? I got held up on the way, and I'm supposed to be meeting someone for dinner tonight——' She glanced at her watch. 'Shall I help you with one of those?'

Utterly bewildered, Amy let her offload the bag from her shoulder. What on earth was Fiona doing here—and why was she being so nice to her?

She followed automatically as Fiona led the way to her car, and got into the passenger seat. Fiona turned to her with a smile as she started the engine. 'You must want to know what all this is about.'

Amy couldn't help noticing that Fiona's left hand, resting on the steering-wheel, was ringless. 'I did wonder,' she said uncertainly. 'I was beginning to suspect this might be a kidnap plot—except no one would want to kidnap me!'

Fiona laughed. She had a light, attractive laugh, and she was somehow more warm and friendly than Amy had ever imagined she could be.

'That's just where you're wrong—someone does! But I've been told you're a bit unpredictable and I've got to get your solemn promise you won't jump out of the car at the next traffic lights, or run away into the woods when we get to——' She interrupted herself. 'Where we're going!'

Amy had the feeling that she knew...but it *couldn't* be! Surely——

'OK.' Fiona took a deep breath as though about to launch herself off into the explanation. 'Don't blame me for any of this—it's all Julius's fault. This is entirely his idea.' There was an awkward pause, then she went on. 'I know this is all a bit embarrassing—we've hardly met each other—but you don't mind if I just come straight out with it? I suppose you must have heard that the wedding was cancelled?'

'Yes. Well, yes, I did. I'm sorry.' She didn't know whether that was the right thing to say or not.

'Don't be,' her companion replied bluntly. 'Look, Amy, I know all about you and Julius and you don't have to feel bad about it. In fact, you've done me an enormous favour, although you're going to think I'm being a bit unscrupulous when you've heard the whole story...' She paused for a second, and then went on. 'I suppose you must have thought I was a prize bitch when you first met me, walking out on Julius in the middle of a dinner party like that? It's all right—you don't have to answer! Well, I was. But I've got far worse things to confess than that.

'I don't have much of an excuse for any of it, except that I really was in a terrible state at the time. I have to admit I did deliberately do things that would rile Julius because I wanted him to break off our engagement. Only he's so damned reasonable he always saw my point of view, even when he lost his temper, and the nearer and nearer we got to the wedding, the worse it became!'

Amy glanced across at her companion in surprise. 'You wanted *him* to break off the engagement? But if you didn't want to marry him why didn't you break it off?' She thought Fiona looked rather embarrassed.

'It's a rather sordid little story, I'm afraid, and the only person who comes out of it well is Julius. You see, when I first met him I'd just been ditched by another man. And then I found out I was pregnant. I couldn't think what to do. I didn't want to get rid of the baby but I couldn't face my parents. My mother...well, she wouldn't have approved. Then I met Julius at this party, and we really liked each other. I will admit that it did cross my mind that he might be the answer to all my problems, and I did deliberately try to attract him.'

Julius, a prey to a calculated deception? Somehow, Amy didn't think he'd be fooled by something like that. Maybe he had seen through the siren act, but liked what he had found underneath. There *was* something very attractive about Fiona.

'Well, after we'd seen each other for a month or so, I took a gamble, and confessed my situation. Julius said he'd guessed, and had been wondering when I'd get round to telling him. I suppose now he probably felt more sorry for me than in love with me. You know how kind he is. And we did like each other—we still do, believe it or not! It didn't seem impossible at the time that marriage might work out. Anyway, to cut a long story short, we got engaged very quickly, planning to marry a month later—much to the disapproval of my mother. It wasn't that she disapproved of Julius—far from it— but she never does things by halves, and immediately started planning the wedding of the year which we didn't have time for.'

'So what happened?' No wonder Julius had told her nothing of Fiona's story. It would have been difficult to do justice to her. And she had suspected him of being callous towards her!

'A couple of weeks after announcing the engagement, I lost the baby,' Fiona explained. 'Julius was very kind to me then... He said there was no reason why we shouldn't continue with our marriage plans—but now we should take things a bit more slowly—so mother was left to her wedding-of-the-year arrangements after all. And then William suddenly came back into my life. He was devastated to hear I'd found out I was pregnant after he'd left me—and I'd lost our child. There's something between William and me that I don't suppose I'll ever have with anybody else, even if he is a bit of a rat. But

the problem was that we were getting closer and closer
to the wedding—we'd even received a couple of presents—and my mother was in top gear, and although it
sounds a bit cowardly I am actually quite scared of her.
And then it seemed so awful to Julius to say, Well, thanks
for wanting to marry me when I was pregnant but now
I'm not so it's all right and I'm going back to William.

'In the end, the only thing I could think of doing was
getting Julius to see what a worthless person I was, and
then he would break off the engagement. That way he
wouldn't be too upset—he'd just think he'd had a lucky
escape—and...this *is* a bit feeble of me, I'm afraid...my
mother wouldn't blame me when the wedding had to be
cancelled. It did mean she'd blame Julius instead, but
he'd be miles away from her so it couldn't hurt him.'

Amy thought about the way Julius had spoken of
Fiona, defending her the night she had walked out on
the dinner party, saying little that would betray any of
her story even in Spain, when he might have used it to
his advantage. Only once had he expressed any irritation, and that was the night he had kissed her under
the mistletoe in the porch, and guessing now how he had
felt about her she knew she had underestimated him. It
wasn't revenge that had prompted him at all, despite what
he had said. He must have felt torn at the time, between
loyalty to Fiona and his growing love for Amy herself.

'So how did you finally sort it all out?' she asked
slowly. 'How do you know about me?'

'Because Julius told me. By the time he got back from
Spain, I'd actually gone away for a few days with
William—I'm afraid I did it deliberately in a last-ditch
attempt to provoke him. I'd left enough clues for him
to be able to come storming along for a terrible row, but
he didn't. He just waited until I got back to London,
and then asked me quite calmly why I'd gone away.
When I finally got round to explaining he said he'd
suspected for some time that I'd changed my mind and

wondered why I wouldn't tell him. It was all very amicable, and when I said I'd felt terrible he said he'd felt pretty bad too since he'd fallen hopelessly in love with one of his secretaries—"the skinny one with the dark red hair"!'

Amy began to laugh as Fiona added apologetically, 'I hope you don't mind that description—I told him that, the way I remembered you, that didn't do you justice at all, and he said the last time he paid you a compliment you'd been quite unpleasant to him!'

'No. I don't mind at all,' Amy said amenably. She could hear Julius's words in her head.

'Anyway, he told me a bit about what happened in Spain and said that, since I was going to be able to use the fact that he'd fallen in love with somebody else to keep my mother at bay, the least I could do was to explain to you why I was so far from heartbroken about it all. He thinks you ran away from him because you thought you were breaking up his relationship with me.'

'Well, I did. And I did think that.'

Fiona smiled across at her. 'So now you know you haven't I hope you're going to be extremely nice to him. I must say, Amy, you've been a lot more honest about it than I would have been! Off on a trip to Spain with a man like Julius—I don't know how you could have resisted him!'

Thinking about it, she wasn't sure how she'd resisted him either, except that Julius had done a bit of resisting on his own account. The night they'd left the show house in such a hurry, and the way he'd avoided coming into the bedroom to wake her earlier that evening—it all began to make much more sense now. He'd avoided being alone with her except in public places, even arranging that their hotel rooms should be on different floors.

Then they were turning in through some high wrought-iron gates that opened into a long dark drive. Fiona said, 'You will invite me to your wedding, Amy, won't you?'

'What makes you think I'm going to get married?'

Fiona laughed. 'I know someone who just can't wait to ask you!'

They pulled up outside a long, stone-built house, with old-fashioned lattice windows. It wasn't possible to see much more in the dark. Several of the windows on the ground floor were lit.

Fiona, with profuse apologies, insisted that she'd have to leave at once if she was to make her dinner engagement, and sent her love to Julius. 'If you don't mind, of course!' she added. 'Got all your stuff? Just ring the doorbell—he'll answer it eventually. It's difficult to hear if you're at the back of the house. Bye, Amy. I hope you'll be really happy!'

She *was* happy. Ecstatically happy, as she watched the tail-lights of Fiona's car disappear behind a belt of trees round a bend in the drive.

She turned towards the house. The front door was made of stout old oak, with a little window of bottle glass in it. There was no light in the hall, although a warm glow spilled out of latticed windows to either side, from behind drawn curtains.

She rang the bell. There was no evidence that anything had happened, so she rang it again. Fiona had said it was difficult to hear, and there was an awful lot of house for the sound to get lost in. She was consumed with impatience. It seemed like a lifetime since she and Julius had been together in Spain.

After a few minutes' wait she tried the bell again. Still no response.

She turned the door-handle experimentally. It was an old iron ring that lifted a latch inside, but when she pushed the door nothing happened. There must be a lock as well. Where was he? Had he forgotten she was coming? On a cold February evening, already dark, he couldn't be expecting any visitors—except herself—and a house standing in its own grounds well away from the road would be vulnerable.

That gave her an idea. The prospect of a cold, indefinite wait on the doorstep didn't appeal at all. Leaving her bags, she began to walk along the front of the house. There must be at least one other entrance—a pity Charlie wasn't with her. He'd visited enough times to know his way about. Somewhere inside the house she heard a dog barking. At least somebody had heard her.

Then she saw the window. It was just open, secured by a long metal catch over a pin on the sill. It wasn't difficult to slip her fingers up on the inside of the frame and push the metal strip up off its peg.

The sill was higher than she would have liked, but it wasn't difficult to scramble up the wall, once she had a firm grip on the raised edge of the window. It was just as well she was wearing her jeans. She hauled herself on to the outside ledge, pushing festoons of creeper out of the way as she did so, to lean precariously through the open frame head first. She brushed one of the curtains aside to look in—no one was there.

It was in precisely that awkward position, head inside the room and bottom outside, that she heard footsteps on the stone paving that ran along the front of the house, coming from the direction of the front door. Twisting herself round with difficulty, she managed to look out again just as the footsteps halted.

He was a few feet away from her, illuminated by the glow from the window. He seemed taller than she'd remembered. He was casually dressed and wore no coat—he must have come from inside the house. There was a half-smile on that rather long, handsome face, the dark eyebrows raised slightly in question.

The silence lengthened while they looked at each other. Amy couldn't tell what she was feeling—a mixture of happiness and excitement, with a terrible doubt that now ne had seen her again he might not really want her any more.

'Most people try the front door,' he said at last.

Despite a very abnormal heartbeat all of a sudden, she tried to sound equally casual. If he didn't seem ecstatic about their first meeting in over a month, she wasn't going to either.

'I did,' she said.

He continued to look at her. 'I suppose breaking and entering might indicate a certain desperation for my company?'

This certainly wasn't the kind of romantic reunion she'd been imagining. He sounded much too cool to be the impatient lover she had been hoping for, and her position—both uncomfortable and inelegant—put her at a distinct disadvantage.

'I haven't broken anything.'

His mouth twitched. 'There was a Rockingham china dog on that windowsill given to me by my eldest niece. Is it still there?'

Contorting herself once again, she examined the sill. It was. Just. She moved it gingerly away from the edge.

'I think I'm stuck,' she said. 'Julius—aren't you a *bit* pleased to see me?'

All he said was, 'Wait there.' And then he vanished round the side of the house.

The window was too small and deeply set in the old stone wall of the house to leave much room for manoeuvre. It was also further from the floor on the inside than she'd imagined.

When he came into the room, she was still kneeling on the sill. She said awkwardly, 'I can't get down with all this clutter—I'm afraid of knocking it off on to the floor. Do you think you could remove your precious dog?'

He did. And several other china ornaments that seemed valuable. Then he came back to stand by the

window, and they looked at each other again. He h▨
made no move to touch her. She wanted to be in h▨
arms, but despite what she thought she knew about his
feelings for her she wasn't sure what to do.

Then he said, 'You've got dead leaves in your hair. I
knew you were trouble from the day I met you. I should
never have given you a job. Where's Fiona?'

'She had to go to dinner with someone. She sent her
love to you. She wants to come to the——' And she
stopped herself just in time. He hadn't even asked her
yet! And maybe, despite what Fiona said, he wasn't going
to.

He was watching her closely. 'And are you convinced
now that her heart isn't broken? And that I'm not
abandoning her callously in favour of you?'

'I never thought you were callous,' she said quickly.
'It was just——'

'I know what it was,' he interrupted. 'You don't need
to explain.'

'But I do!' she insisted earnestly. 'That was why I had
to lie to you about the way I felt . . .'

Why was he looking at her like that? 'Until then,' he
said slowly, 'I was never really sure what your feelings
were—just when I'd decided I'd got it all worked out,
you'd act so cool and ordinary again that I'd think I
was wrong.'

'I never tried to make you love me, Julius! I didn't
want you to——'

'I know. The world's most reluctant enchantress. But
I told you, sweetheart—I understand.' That one en-
dearment did strange things to her, and she began to feel
that ecstatic glow again. 'I don't suppose,' he was saying,
'just to set the record straight, you'd like to tell me the
truth this time?'

'Until then,' he had said; until she had lied to him . . .
Her mouth curved into a beautifully witchy smile.

What makes you think I love you?' she demanded
.tly, 'Why didn't you believe what I told you in
Granada?'

'Because I knew you well enough to be able to detect
an outright lie. Your eyes go glassy.'

The Charlie look... How very humiliating!

'So we needn't have been apart all this time...'

He took a step towards the window, so close now,
they were almost touching. 'I would have tried to explain it to you that day I phoned you, if you'd waited
around long enough to listen.'

'Were you very angry with me for walking out like
that at the office?'

'I wasn't exactly pleased about it...'

She looked so abashed that he began to laugh. Then
he put his hands round her waist and pulled her towards
him off the windowsill into his arms, kissing her face
and then her mouth.

Her arms went round his neck as he gathered her
closer, and she gave a long sigh. 'Why did that take you
so long?'

He slid one hand up under her jacket, while the other
stroked her hair. 'I was beginning to be afraid you might
have changed your mind since Granada.' He kissed her
ear. 'So you *do* love me?'

'Yes,' she said. 'I do. Very, very much.'

They didn't speak for a long time after that. Then his
eyes, that wonderful lucid grey, looked down into hers.
He was smiling. 'What were you going to tell me about
Fiona?'

She avoided answering directly—they still hadn't got
round to the vital question.

Then, because she complained she was hungry, they
found their way to the kitchen and a 'Welcome home,
Amy' dinner which had been delivered earlier that day
by Jess, courtesy of Cookery Unlimited.

'You've all been very busy conspiring behind my back, haven't you?' she accused. 'First Celia and Fiona, and now my best friend! Where *are* the treacherous Baileys?'

'Jess is still at your cottage with Charlie, and Celia's at home. They both insisted that I remind you that you never said anything about not telling me which train you were on.'

'I forgive them,' she offered magnanimously. 'And what's Charlie been up to?'

'Nothing. Except he wants to ask you if Rasputin can come to the wedding.'

'Oh,' she said. And then, carelessly, 'Whose wedding?'

'Ours.'

A typical Julius assumption, that—and he hadn't even asked her!

And typical again that before she'd even opened her mouth to point it out he was on to another subject. 'Your family has a strange way with names——'

'What makes you say that?'

'Well, among other things, why on earth did you call a respectable English tabby after a Russian monk of doubtful character?'

What *other things*? 'My mother used to think he had mesmeric eyes.'

'They're not mesmeric,' he said shortly. 'They're crossed.'

She kissed his chin and stared up at him adoringly. 'That's a pity,' she said, 'because they remind me a bit of yours.'

They took the elaborate meal into a small sitting-room at the back of the house, where there was a fire alight in the wide old hearth. A very young red setter lay in front of it, and leapt up in demented welcome at Julius's appearance.

'She's Charlie's,' he explained. 'I hope you don't mind. She was a present from my sister Sally before she

...ved into her own house. We've only had her a couple ...months, so she's still a bit of a delinquent.'

Amy laughed as the animal licked enthusiastically at her face. 'She's lovely! What's her name?'

It was the pause, as well as the choice of phrase, that gave it away. 'We're ... still discussing it.'

And that was typical Charlie! She was very amused. Her eyes, a wicked blue, met his. 'One of the "other things" you mentioned? I don't mind!'

'But I do!' he said firmly. 'I'm not having my wife's brother yelling for a dog that has the same name as my wife—even if he does call it *Ames*. "Amy" means beloved—it's a beautiful name and it's going to stay that way!' The tone of his voice belied the humour in his eyes, something that was very familiar to her now.

'So what's he calling it now?' she asked curiously.

'Jess.'

The conversation degenerated after that.

They had dinner by candlelight, and a discussion on the topic of Cookery Unlimited prompted her to ask doubtfully, 'I suppose you think I ought to give up cooking and devote myself entirely to you?'

'I don't think anything of the sort! Darling, I want you to be happy. Do whatever you like—I mean it. It's up to you where we live—and if you want to stay down here permanently and run the business from here there's a cottage in the grounds we could do up for Jess and you can both start a gastronomic revolution in Wiltshire. Charlie has great plans for the cellars since he found out about home-made wines from Sally.'

She groaned. 'That's all we need!'

Julius put his arms round her, pulling her close. 'Don't worry, I'll see that he doesn't get into any trouble. I don't want you to have to worry about Charlie—or anything—from now on. All right?'

'All right.' After a while, she said, 'There's something I've wondered about for a long time—you know that day you found me asleep in the church porch?'

'The Sleeping Beauty stunt?'

'It wasn't a stunt!' she protested indignantly. 'I was exhausted! Anyway, I had this dream. You didn't, I suppose, kiss me . . . did you?'

He traced a line down her nose with one finger, and then the contours of her mouth. 'I don't usually go round kissing the kind of people who fall asleep in church porches—or who climb in through people's windows for that matter—though it did cross my mind!' There was a pause. 'Talking of kissing . . .'

'Mm,' she agreed, her eyes meeting his. 'But there's just one thing I'd like you to know first, Julius Prior——'

'What's that?'

'You haven't actually *asked* me to marry you.'

There was a surprised silence. 'I haven't?'

'No,' she said firmly. 'And I think it's time someone pointed out to you that people do like to be asked things rather than told them!'

One dark eyebrow was raised in genuine amazement. 'But you are going to marry me, aren't you?'

And somehow, after that, there really wasn't much point in waiting for a more appropriately phrased question! She gave a sigh, and managed to sound convincingly resigned. 'I suppose I'll have to, since Fiona was so keen on coming to the wedding—I thought she could sit beside Jacquie and Zoe . . .'

He laughed and pushed her back on the sofa, and all of a sudden she found herself trapped by his weight, as his lips burned impatient little kisses in a trail across the side of her face to her mouth. She could only just get her next words out—and they were her last, for quite some time . . .

'It'd make their year . . . !'

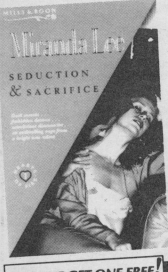

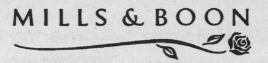

MILLS & BOON

Forthcoming Titles

DUET
Available in April

The Betty Neels Duet **A SUITABLE MATCH**
THE MOST MARVELLOUS SUMMER

The Emma Darcy Duet **PATTERN OF DECEIT**
BRIDE OF DIAMONDS

FAVOURITES
Available in April

NOT WITHOUT LOVE Roberta Leigh
NIGHT OF ERROR Kay Thorpe

LOVE ON CALL
Available in April

VET IN A QUANDARY Mary Bowring
NO SHADOW OF DOUBT Abigail Gordon
PRIORITY CARE Mary Hawkins
TO LOVE AGAIN Laura MacDonald

Next Month's Romances

Each month you can choose from a wide variety of romance with Mills & Boon. Below are the new titles to look out for next month, why not ask either Mills & Boon Reader Service or your Newsagent to reserve you a copy of the titles you want to buy – just tick the titles you would like and either post to Reader Service or take it to any Newsagent and ask them to order your books.

Please save me the following titles: **Please tick**   ✓

Title	Author	
AN UNSUITABLE WIFE	Lindsay Armstrong	
A VENGEFUL PASSION	Lynne Graham	
FRENCH LEAVE	Penny Jordan	
PASSIONATE SCANDAL	Michelle Reid	
LOVE'S PRISONER	Elizabeth Oldfield	
NO PROMISE OF LOVE	Lilian Peake	
DARK MIRROR	Daphne Clair	
ONE MAN, ONE LOVE	Natalie Fox	
LOVE'S LABYRINTH	Jessica Hart	
STRAW ON THE WIND	Elizabeth Power	
THE WINTER KING	Amanda Carpenter	
ADAM'S ANGEL	Lee Wilkinson	
RAINBOW ROUND THE MOON	Stephanie Wyatt	
DEAR ENEMY	Alison York	
LORD OF THE GLEN	Frances Lloyd	
OLD SCHOOL TIES	Leigh Michaels	

If you would like to order these books in addition to your regular subscription from Mills & Boon Reader Service please send £1.90 per title to: Mills & Boon Reader Service, Freepost, P.O. Box 236, Croydon, Surrey, CR9 9EL, quote your Subscriber No:.................................. (If applicable) and complete the name and address details below. Alternatively, these books are available from many local Newsagents including W H Smith, J Menzies, Martins and other paperback stockists from 8 April 1994.

Name:..

Address:..

....Post Code:.........................

To Retailer: If you would like to stock M&B books please contact your regular book/magazine wholesaler for details.